1st Edition published 1997

Copyright 1976

ISBN 1-55056-541-9

Published by:

In Canada: Golden Bell Publishing House Inc.
P.O. Box 2680
Grand Forks, B.C. V0H 1H0

In US: Golden Bell Publishing House Inc.
P.O. Box 181
Danville, Washington 99121-0181

PRINTED
IN CANADA

CONTENTS

Chapter I

The Finding

Curling smoke drifted atop the huge cedar trees and heavy, as if laden with the burden of the shortcomings of man, it began to submerge beneath the tips, the crowns of the trees, chasing the wildlife in disarray all over the holy ground of Altan Tobchi.

The horses of the two men exhibited increased anxiety the moment they left the cover of the forest. In front of them lay the charred wooden beams pointing morbidly into the pale sky: a skeleton of despair and horror. The huge bell, once tied, swayed sadly amid the chaos. The horses had been forced to halt at first; but then, after the riders had observed long enough, they cautioned the animals to continue in the direction where the ruins lay, aiming toward the Great Hall, whatever was left of it. Having lost all its walls to the hellish torch, it stood as a monument to the miraculous power of destruction which must have ruled the previous day. The wind drifted to the north and only a small amount of the acrid smoke touched the travellers. At about half the distance which it took to reach the former hall, the men would stop their horses one more time. It was now that they began to see the first signs of a horror which had reigned here only but a short while ago. Dozens of lifeless bodies displayed themselves to the brethren in the way in which they had been caught at the moment of their demise, accepting their destiny, showing either the engraved signs of

1

struggle or the submissive power of surprise etched into their faces. It appeared that the ones who were not burned had been shot while others seemed to have been marauded then killed in a senseless slaughter and left to the demise of the flames. Bits of cloth stuck to the swollen corpses which, robbed of their covering, lay pitifully on the charred ground, their legs twisted over fallen debris, their heads disfigured: some smiling, in contrast, rather peacefully as they were overcome by such intrusion. The two riders remained motionless where they stood. The Manchurian finally broke the silence turning his horse to slowly move to the far side of the grounds in order to comprehend the scene from a different viewpoint. Separated as they now were, each man dealt with the visual impressions in his very own personal way as the chaotic scene became a part of the world of both riders. Never had they witnessed close-up such a senseless killing, a carnage which would defy man as being the messenger of God: he who was sent to arrange for peace, watching over the bounty of the earth so that all life could blossom as the Creator had hoped. The leftover debris told of a storm of rage which unleashed itself here, incinerated by depraved minds whose inferno stems from the abyss of hatred. A paradise torn from the hinges of heaven lay here ravaged before them while the exhausted breath of the leftover mayhem began to unbalance the still standing pillars: one of them swaying in the undulating air current, ready to fall if it would please the gods.

As the empty sky began to wake up this new day, the sun was shining through vaporous clouds drawing themselves from nowhere across the lost firmament. The White Priest followed his friend and was the first to dismount. Hesitantly, sliding from where he was, he landed near his horse balancing elastically on his feet while turning around. He began to walk over some still burning beams which lay scattered about the ground. As they offered a hazard to his advancement, it was the Manchurian who voiced some advice of caution to his friend. The White Priest began slowly to make his way atop the remnants of the center of the Great Hall. Here a portion of the wall was still intact, erect but leaning dangerously toward the outside of the enclosure, ready to collapse should the shifting wind catch it unprepared. The awesome looking scene held little hope and offered no blessings from the past. Time appeared to stand still framing the deeds of enraged beings within this moment. It would be its forgiving nature to soon cover the site with new greenery and restore peace once more. Nothing could be done here. The White Priest wandered aimlessly, disturbing a few hot embers whose grey and black dust left puffs of air and smoldering coals to wrestle with each other over the supremacy of marking the spot which was hotter than the rest, trying to establish what had happened between yesterday and this day, a time which had come and now seemingly had passed over the wake of destruction. His counterpart, the Manchurian, had done likewise. At some point he had unsheathed his sword as he walked away from the threshold of his beloved foundry, crossing the little bridge which led to the Great Hall. Both men had ended their walk and had the desire to meet away from the ghastly pictures which offered themselves in all directions.

"The sword will not help you here any longer," began the younger man, the White Priest, finding his friend still clutching his weapon as he approached him.

3

"It may no longer help but this blade shall certainly never forget!" replied the friend who had now drawn close enough for the younger one to understand his frustration.

"Let's see whether they found what they were after," the younger brother pointed uphill as he spoke to where the treasure was waiting for anyone who knew of its existence.

"You mean the gold?" uttered the Manchurian quietly.

"Yes," said his friend while already beginning to mount his horse. Slowly directing it away from where he was, he aimed for the spot where the creek concealed the yellow metal.

The Japanese friend did likewise, following the direction of the first horse. Soon both animals halted and the riders scanned the ground. There was no sign revealing that any intruder had gone further uphill.

"How strange! They already turned around here," remarked the first of the two riders.

"We should see whether we can account for all the brethren. Perhaps they captured some and took them along in order to return at a later time?" The Manchurian looked backward as he spoke as if to underline the fact that the situation behind them deserved more attention than anything else.

"You're right, Takuan. Let's bury them and see whether we can find out anything more down there." And in so saying, the White Priest turned his horse around followed by his friend who had his sword now sheathed, tied behind his back crossing it in such a way that the hilt could only be seen from the front, protruding slightly between his neck and his ear.

Thus, as they began to slowly organize themselves and settle their emotions, they were now ready to spend some time on the grounds in order to look after their slain friends.

"They used automatic weapons, Takuan," resumed the younger of the two men the conversation which continued only sparingly.

The Japanese nodded slightly turning to his friend, "Seven bullets I counted across the chest of one of the Tibetans."

The horses bounced the riders slowly around as they rode into the advanced morning, downhill to once more tread on the holy ground of Altan Tobchi. The Manchurian had taken the lead. While passing his younger friend, he gave him the first faint smile since they had practiced with their swords sometime ago.

"I will call you the White Tiger," he said. "You are white: you are as tense as a tiger and you are also as calm as one." Pausing here for a moment, he continued, "And you are equally as quick and strong in what you are doing."

"Hmm...a human tiger?" sighed the other man telling his friend that a human being has nothing in common with a tiger whatsoever. "Man reaches three times the tiger's age yet learns very little of what is essential to understand nature. No my friend, I may act like one but there are many things which I will never learn from a tiger."

"And what might that be?" queried the Manchurian while holding his horse back as if this would assist him in better understanding a potentially difficult answer.

"That, Takuan, is a very simple secret the tiger himself will not tell his dear human friend, you see?"

"Yes I do understand..Tiger."

5

The young man used a short hand motion to ridicule their conversation denoting that it was nothing of importance for it began to embarrass him; but he smiled just the same. However, the mood of both men was in no way a relaxed one. The few smiles they exchanged were feeble and generated by sheer desperation and confusion. They had tried to count the hoofs on the ground hoping to establish how many bandits had come here; but at best they could only estimate that twenty or thirty horses participated in the raid.

"They must have struck here like lightning!" resumed the Manchurian, shaking his head in disbelief.

"Yes," answered the younger one, "like a thousand thunderbolts!"

The horses were trotting along, descending, when the Manchurian made a hissing sound, "Down from your horse quick! Over there ... several riders to the left on the tree line."

Such a warning was followed by swift action. Both men were off their animals before the warning had ended. They quickly pulled their horses a few yards back behind the covering growth of some tall bushes. Bewildered by the rapid change and moreover sensing the excitement, the animals were not too cooperative; but soon the calming voices of their masters accomplished the rest. The White Tiger gave the reins to his friend who held the horses, forcing them further to the side behind even higher bushes.

"It's two of the Mongols!" observed the young one. "They're continuing toward the far side of the hill. It doesn't appear that they've spotted us." Pausing here for a few seconds the young man resumed, "...and they have automatic rifles,"pausing again, he then added quietly, "..both of them."

"What do they want here now?" came the angry question from the Manchurian. "There's nothing left to look forward to, everything and everyone has been burned to the ground!"

The two distant riders proceeded about their business, easing their horses alongside the margin of the forest, seemingly unconcerned, almost sickeningly carefree.

The early morning sun was becoming noticeably warmer as it climbed upward into the azure blue sky which seemed to swallow the fog and clouds alike. Regardless of the warmth, it was a habit of the Mongols to wear furry hats. The adornment was becoming: it lent beauty as well as harshness to their presence. The two monks were unable to get a good look at them but just the same, their deportment, the type of horses they rode and the dress they wore, they were Mongols all right - maybe not bandits but in the face of what had recently transpired the monks were not eager to take any chances.

"We should tie up our horses and make for over there!" The Manchurian pointed in the direction he wanted to go.

"Yeah, and then what? What should we do over there? What if the horses are spotted and what if we're unable to get back to them? I can't outbox two riflemen at the same time! Remember, they can throw bullets faster and farther than we're able to throw our punches, my friend Takuan!"

The Japanese hummed under his breath. It was not a specific tune though it most certainly sounded like one. Takuan always hummed this peculiar melody whenever he was confronted with something new, something which would excite him.

The day emitted a strange warmth which was more that of

a false spring day but as the summer was already far advanced the dampness and that sort of cooling drift which hung in the air was more like the sign of an early fall. The spring and the fall seasons shared this strange characteristic of weather as if nature was showing unison where men failed to show compassion. *"Everything moves in cycles,"* said the Master of the young Tiger once. *"Somewhere it must balance."* Yes the Yin and the Yang had their origin in nature and that most certainly was the source from which Master Fu Yen as well must have taken his observation.

Both monks decided to wait it out under the protective cover of the tall bushes. In the meantime, the Mongolian riders reached the far side of the hill. They had made certain sudden stops and on occasion they even left their mounts all by themselves in order to examine one or the other dead bodies more closely. Because of the distance, it was almost impossible for the two monks to accurately observe what they were actually doing. It was difficult for the men in hiding to imagine the unimaginable. But then again, just before the horses had reached an even level with the two watching friends, they were able to get another good view of the riders.

"One of them is holding some sort of paper, a map it looks like," whispered the Manchurian.

In fact they were turning the paper around while at the same time changing positions. Their horses, in disagreement, showed their displeasure whenever the reins were pulled to ensure that they follow the course of their search. The short Mongolian horses are stalky, rough looking runners which do not enjoy the strict command of a small circle turn. It was possible that should one of them begin to neigh, the animals which the two monks had tied up would answer the call of the herd. By the same token, the Mongolians had come too high up the hill and if they decided to continue climbing in the way they had done till now, it was only a matter of time before both brothers, Takuan as well as his *"Tiger"* friend, would be jeopardizing their safety. Of course, they could slowly withdraw down the hill in the cover of the small trees and the underbrush thus losing sight of the intruders but remaining themselves undetected. As the time had arrived to do something very quickly both men elected to follow the latter action. Leading their animals away and down the hill they soon lost sight of the Mongolians, a thought which neither of the two friends particularly relished. Once they had removed themselves from the immediate zone of danger, the men stopped.

"We should leave our horses here and hike back to see what they're up to," and in so proposing the younger man slipped off his horse and began to tie it up.

Takuan agreed, doing the same. Within the next few minutes both men proceeded to work their way back up the hill which they not too long ago had left. After they covered about half the original distance, the Manchurian caught sight of the fur hat of one of the foreign riders. Touching his friend on the shoulder, he successfully warned him of the impending danger. The warriors on top had begun to follow what appeared to be the trail of the horses of the two monks. This was indeed dangerous and could only result in a confrontation within a very short time. The small path leading downhill was well marked by the tracks their animals had left. The Mongolians were masters in reading such imprints embedded in the soil. Leaving the reins dangling atop their saddles, they had their hands free as they rode toward the two monks. Hand signs can be easily understood: they are remarkably explicit and dramatic especially if given in a moment of danger. Little time was left to plan or even ponder what would be most beneficial, either to mislead the Mongols or attack them - or trick them and then attack them. Both friends had jumped away from the path - skillfully avoiding marking the ground. Leaping across the grassy portion, one of them positioned himself behind a huge tree while the other actually climbed into a medium sized oak whose foliage provided ample cover. It was the White Priest who had chosen to be above the intruders.

Soon the first dull sounds of the pounding hoofs drumming on the firm sandy ground vibrated up into the trunk of the oak tree. On the other side of the pathway the Manchurian prepared himself. His sword now left its safe cover and the cold steel was unsheathed...waiting. The Mongols were not interested in their paper any longer: the one which they had studied as they crossed the devastated land. Their eyes were very much pinned to the ground. Suddenly, one of them halted his horse. Glancing toward the grassy soil, he detected the change which the grass would reveal to anyone capable of understanding certain rules of nature. Once stepped or trodden upon, the tiny shoots do not immediately spring back into their original positions. However, anything could bend a dozen or so grass stems. The luring, big tracks made by the horses seemed to win over the more insignificant ones. The riders continued in their pursuit. Soon after though, one of the horsemen stopped his animal again. He had by now reached the oak tree in

10

which the White Tiger was hiding. The young priest observed how his enemy below him unshouldered his rifle. It was of an old war vintage which he must have traded away from some Soviet expedition of which there were plenty. At times, the Russians would sell weapons for certain favours, vodka or Mongol maids. The warrior nomads would supply anything within reason. Lately, however, the Red government had declared war on the bandits themselves which accounted for the fact that they, as well, were withdrawing into the dense cover of the distant wilderness. Hence, this confrontation here and now. The second Mongol rider was still a few paces back. The White Priest hesitated. Should he leap in front of the first rider or should he wait until his horse was directly beneath him? What if one of them would dismount and search further? The tracks on the grass most definitely would lead them to both their hiding places, and once warned, the Mongols surely would approach uncertainty with drawn guns. That much was clear in the mind of the hidden observer! At this very moment while still caught in the grip of indecision, the first rider began to move forward again....one...two...three, four, five...NOW! A shadow dropped from above the first rider and a crushing blow landed on the side of the neck of the shocked intruder. His horse veered to the side, rearing high in the air, losing finally its burden. Both men fell to the ground but only one of them was ready to continue the fight. The second Mongol had reached for his gun and was just about to line it up. He did not need to aim but simply straighten the barrel in order to mow his opponent down. It was at that moment when a silvery steel beam shot threw midair, followed by silence. One might hear a feather drop: a dull, thumping sound and the

11

length of the steel bored itself deep into the chest of the second rider, the hilt on top swaying to and fro until it found its balance and stood like a marker, straight, reaching out and diagonally upward into the sky which had nothing in common with the happenings. Shortly after, the body began to lean to one side then slid to the ground. The horse did not have time to alter its position: it had no choice in the matter either. The Manchurian stepped from behind the trunk which had provided him the necessary cover for his attack. Facing each other, they had no immediate words. The Tiger walked toward the latter Mongolian rider who still had the sword deep in his chest and who by then had already made peace with the rest of the world. Takuan as well walked slowly toward the man. He touched him with his shoe and turned him slightly to the side. Then, placing his foot on the dead man's chest, he reached for his sword, grabbed it with both hands and pulled the weapon free. The two Mongolian horses were standing alongside the morbid scene, one hanging its head, the other gazing aimlessly into the distance as if the only thing which mattered was to return back there from whence it had come, to the green meadows beneath the brown hills where the yurts would be left empty tonight...and countless others to come. Both animals carried saddles. The brothers had horses which were not as well grown and equipped. A saddle out here was something only a king could afford, and...there were no kings any longer, at least no living ones. While the two began to exchange words more excitement was about to come their way. On top of the hill they sighted a lance which was stuck in the trunk of a tree and stood like a giant marker.

"We better get that thing down fast!" cautioned the

Manchurian, quickly mounting the nearest horse and storming against the steep hill. His friend observed him as he arrived, twisting the shaft from out of the huge trunk and breaking the shank of the weapon such that the sound of splintering wood could be heard a hundred or more steps away. It was as if someone spoke of justice: it was as if some unforeseen force had avenged the intruders; yet it felt, just the same, as if more disgrace had befallen the holy grounds. Altan Tobchi was no longer standing and the lance, with its coloured ribbon, had gone as well. His work finished, the wild Manchurian flew back down the hill. Soon his friend, whom he respectfully called Tiger, would get a firsthand look into the staccato eyes of Takuan which were gleaming with flashes of cobalt, sparking away at the world when he finally brought his mount under abrupt control, whirling the dirt about and forcing the horse almost to the ground. The friend was a helpless onlooker conscious only of the bravura which he had just witnessed. "Get on your horse and cut the others loose. Chase them away. Come on, hurry! There are another twenty or more of them riding uphill from the bridge." His young friend flung himself onto the stallion and being for the first time solidly planted in their saddles, both men ensured their animals were well scattered. Then they left under the dense cover of the underbrush to make for the crest of the hill, descending on the far side along the same route which the Invited Spirit had once been brought to join the lost paradise of Altan Tobchi. Neither man would ever return here. They seemed to sense this as they aimed into the distance, upward. At this point, they did not worry about their horses but urged them on as much as the animals would allow. Before they began to

13

descend both men stopped their horses, looking backward one more time. The carefree Mongolians, however, had not changed their pace as they lazily trotted in groups across the still smouldering site. The right hand of the Japanese flew into the air and there it remained for a few seconds only, following the code of the Lost Jade. His friend as well acknowledged the meaning of this gesture and repeated the sign which should forever bless and seal the book of this remote monastery to the rest of mankind.

"Down there," pointed the Tiger, "and then left!" While his horse in giant leaps catapulted over the cascading creeks until brought under control again, he remained in the flow of the watershed, followed by the Warrior. From this moment on he would affectionately call his friend the Warrior and the Manchurian would simply continue to refer to the young white man as his friend Tiger.

And so it was that the Tiger and the Warrior rode downhill away from the horrors of the past few days to find a new life in the unknown regions where men reigned much more severely and where no brotherhood knew of sharing in the daily struggle. They had no food: they had no home any longer and they had no protection other than the simple weapons which by good fortune had come their way - the Samurai sword and the Chinese leaf sword, and the skill to go along with them. One of the men wanted to reach the coast which lay east and the other one would attempt to ride toward the west; but, for the moment, they would remain together. Following the stream downward for many hours, it finally was time to rest. Securing their horses, they walked about the immediate area in order to find a suitable resting place. The sun had already set and the counterglow from above warned them that they should prepare for a long, dark and very cool night.

"You see," said the Warrior, "a Mongol never forgets defeat." A fire could therefore not be afforded and only one of the men could sleep. The Warrior asked for the first watch while the young friend took the blankets which were still rolled in front of the saddle and prepared his bed.

Chapter II
A Different World

Equally as a Mongol tribesman never forgets defeat is he, the same warrior fierce and unrelenting in his dealings, loyal to his word. Certain contradictions to this observation have been known to exist throughout the many centuries in which the Great Khan ruled the empire of the Mongols. As great and significant as this may have seemed to be, it would find a quick end in comparison to the known times in which history governed the distribution of lines of interest, that is borders on this globe. The Mongol, having his civilization well tied to his nomadic life, was bound by the very intense laws of nature. The grazing herd would move on. It was here that his livelihood was made and if the drive of the cattle demanded more and fresher grassland the Mongol must follow. Anything of value had to be packed, folded and moved. Little incentive existed and even less time to create anything which might interfere with his moving on. Today no monuments of their civilization survive other than the written word of the days which were recorded in the vellums of the great books - and there they remain: the heritage of the great Mongol tribesmen, the warriors. The earlier group, who some eight hundred years before Genghis Khan left the same kind of mark, stemmed from very similar roots. The Huns under Attila stormed west across the plains until they arrived at the walls of Rome where finally they retreated after the death of their leader. Genghis Khan (meaning the most perfect warrior or very mighty ruler) decided at the age of forty-four to unite his tribes at the Onon River in eastern Siberia. Their habits from then and now exhibit little change. Forced into a new culture, they finally sent their sons to institutions of learning abdicating their lifestyle of aimless wandering and the call of their storming drive to conquer. The Great Khan, Temujin his boyhood name, prided himself over many things, a few of which would brand his character as being that of a man who was ruthless, cruel and who understood the law of fear which travelled ahead of his million-strong horde. Drinking blood and eating the flesh of his watchdogs were only a few of the reported feats during his hardy life. It was said that he ate lice and rats as well and exhibited resistance toward fatigue and extreme temperature in an unparalleled way. Most of the recorded cruelty in history began after Genghis Khan was betrayed by the Shah of Kharismia who beheaded one of his messengers in retaliation. Subsequently, the ancient city of Merv, known for its libraries, was sacked and a million people in the area slaughtered, sparing none. The Great Khan was not a man of his word at all. His treachery should remain unequalled in the history of mankind since. However, after his death, his son Ogotai was unable to secure his conquests and rivalry cut short all the advances which had been drenched by blood and the lust for cruel warfare. The world does not remember him for monuments, art, literature or architectural achievements, but rather for the ruins left by his scorched earth policy of a warfare which was executed more by his *celestials,* the horses he bred according to the great leader of the Huns, Attila. These Fergana horses, with their very hard natural hoofs, would carry the horror

17

westward until the land which was conquered was so gigantic in distance and space that it could not be ruled over any longer. So the warrior nomads drifted along the path of destiny which was in the very beginning already set out for them as in the history of mankind it would be said: *a nomad comes from nowhere and goes to nowhere.* He is drifting with a fate that is tied to the herd.

Thus the Mongol bandits had no true quarrel with the new political direction as long as they could follow their own instinctive drive. They liked their yurts, the felt tents, and no restrictions, no confinement to one place. However, the Chinese government as well as the Soviet administration was opposed to these free wheeling warriors. As it became more difficult by the day to match the modern organized military, it was predictable that the Mongols soon would become a memory only.

The night had lasted long enough. Having the Mongols on their minds, neither of the last residents of Altan Tobchi had slept well. It was not that they distrusted each other's ability to guard but rather their joint awareness of the Mongol's capability to appear when least expected. Fortunately, they had not shown up and thus the new day began totally on its own merits. Eating time, as it would have been on the mountain, had arrived - but for the first time they had no food. This also might have been one of the reasons why they did not sleep too well. As the very early morning proceeded to announce itself and as the dew began to gnaw away at their sparse clothing, penetrating it with its dampness and other equally well known properties, the two were already busy establishing certain priorities. Firstly, no matter how they might look upon it, the time had come to think of the most important of all problems confronting them - namely that of food. Rolling his blanket up, it was the White Priest who chose to elaborate upon this very grim situation saying that they had no maps or anything of the sort in order to identify their whereabouts. The Warrior pointed toward the east as if this was a better subject to discuss.

"I have to go that way, to the land of the rising sun," while he, as well, was gathering his belongings and placing them back on his horse.

"It is not the land of the rising sun any longer, my friend," answered the Tiger causing the Japanese to listen more closely than he normally would.

"You don't think so?" replied the Manchurian and upon asking as to why his friend would believe this he got his answer.

"You as well have lost the war. You actually lost the war in more than one way, against the Chinese primarily but then also against the Soviets."

"You call that a war with Russia?" retorted his brother who had spent eighteen months with him in the monastery. "They only declared war against us in the last weeks of the conflict!"

"Precisely!" replied his friend who now interrupted his activity in order to give some extra emphasis to his words. "That is why they will ask for reparation monies and if there are none..for land."

At this very moment the call of a bush chicken (quail) interrupted their conversation. The Manchurian reacted to the sign of silence given him by his friend while the latter dropped everything. Reaching for his throwing knife, a straight steel blade which had lost its wooden handle, he leapt over the many different natural obstacles and caught the chattering bird in an uproar. The weapon had been thrown with sufficient thrust certainly; nevertheless, it had missed and the noisy animal scurried away awakening the rest of the forest. It was just as well. Upon his return from the *hunting trip*, it was the Manchurian who smiled faintly. It was not because the breakfast had escaped them but rather the fact that it did.

"I know," said the young man who had just learned that hunting can be a full time profession. "I guess I'm not too good at it!"

Both men would soon find out that the protected ways on the distant hill of Altan Tobchi had disappeared for good. The many wonderful things which one finds only in such places and within the restful, complacent pages of holy scriptures cannot be readily established nor can they be easily maintained. A monk would never kill game, even a domesticated animal. They would consume milk, honey from the living, but they would never kill first and then eat. Both men discovered simultaneously that the essential act of surviving knew very little about such habits. It was not difficult for them to return to their old ways, the ones with which they were already familiar before entering Altan Tobchi. The long, cold night and the previous days had taken their toll. Hungry and cold, tired and nervous, the once steady hand relinquished all that which the mind was able to attain. It was the mind, its disorder, that had already affected the calmness of its guiding force. Here, somewhere, lay buried the age-old drive which governs all men when taken prisoner by circumstances such as the two had been presented with against their will. Readying themselves for the ride, they looked from their vantage point down the hill several miles to the road which they called the trading way and on which they had travelled numerous times. Yes, a new adventure lay before them equally as gigantic as this land mass, overwhelming and vast, with blazing deserts and towering mountain ranges, luscious valleys and gardens of eternal bliss, all of which was encompassed in one name - *Asia*.

The last part of the path which led them to the trading route was steep and more treacherous than the entire trip had been since they had left the hill. Extreme caution was required. The Mongols knew the territory well and it stood to reason that they could presume what the two would do. Holding their horses back, they avoided the path itself which began to drop sharply. It was the spot where they always dismounted: one of the monks would lead the animals into the river bed and the rest of the group would then follow the shorter road downward which always allowed for a substantial time difference between the two parties. The White Priest led his friend. Both followed the large creek and before reaching the entrance to the road they proceeded to tie up their horses. It was time to take a very careful look! After securing their mounts well both men travelled the last portion on foot.

The Manchurian, walking in front, speculated, "It's best if I show my face on the road first. Most cannot distinguish us from the Chinese. You, my friend," he laughingly added, "look more like a Russian who has lost his way!"

His friend agreed and so they went about their task which was to reach the road and seek out the best cover, concealed behind the huge underbrush and the enormous trunks of the cedar trees. As they had spent several minutes in this endeavour, it was the Manchurian who now entered the road to take a *reading* as to the evidence which the travellers would have left in the event that someone had been here just recently. Walking to and fro between the two sides of the road he seemed to be satisfied with his findings. Returning to his sheltered place, he confronted his friend, "Nothing, only motor vehicles, trucks and the sort," came the sonorous voice of the disappointed man.

Noticing this, the young friend began to question his mood further. "Only motor tracks, you mean spoors of cars or trucks?"

"Yes," verified the Manchurian calmly.

"You better start to think. There's a revolution being fought here, remember?" The Japanese acted as if he had forgotten the past days of a war in which he had been involved for many years. A lazy arm movement added to the already impressive way in which his mannerisms displayed themselves, claiming that all was over since they, the Japanese, had lost the war.

The young friend reminded him of the stories which they had heard about the Chinese now battling furiously amongst themselves. It had been established in the past that the Soviets actually aided the Red Chinese against the group calling themselves the Kuomintang, the Nationalists. "The tracks which you've sighted could easily be those of the Soviet transports for the cadres of the other Chinese. One of our brethren told us he'd seen guns on this road, an entire convoy of them, remember?" His Tiger was extremely convincing as he continued, "You see, at the moment they don't particularly mind a Russian face but boy if they find a Japanese here I can assure you they will not be as lenient!"

22

The otherwise calm Warrior straightened himself before answering, "But, we have no guns and no ammunition!"

"- and -" his friend falling into his sentence continued, "and most of all no food!"

Their saddlebags contained an iron ration which they would only touch once they had eaten no food for three full days. On this the men had agreed beforehand. After an uncomfortable period of silence, it was the Manchurian who began to speak of the necessity to formulate a plan. Firstly, he had to travel east which was in direct contradiction to his friend's desire to move westward. Finally, they agreed that they both would travel south until they reached the Old Silk Road. Both knew it existed but neither had any precise idea regarding where and how to reach it. The Sayan Range, secluded as it was, had in the not too distant surroundings larger towns. It was only the remoteness and the hostility of the land which separated them from the prying eyes of searchers who came in many different forms of the human species: either as hunters, adventurers (a more seldom found breed of men alike the bandits) or government expeditionary forces - many of them had been sighted and many more were in the planning stages. Oil, silver, gold and ores of other valuable properties were continually being discovered. The industrial age had begun to close in and the forgotten land was being prepared for modern conquest. Just the same, amidst all this, time seemed to stand still. Whenever one expedition left, the same desolate quietness returned as if nothing at all had transpired. In the face of this, both friends agreed on their first step in a journey which would bring them halfway around the world.

"Our brothers went as far as the Hatgal crossing avoiding the east side of the great lake," said the Japanese.

"How did they ever survive on the other side in that wilderness?" asked his friend.

"They didn't have to," came the answer back.

"- and how did they do that?"

"Simple, my friend, by boat," prompted the Manchurian. The White Priest accepted his boat story because there was nothing more plausible. The imminent question was however: *Where could a boat be had?* After a brief discussion and much more deliberation, it was clear to both friends that they would have to find a boat meaning: they had to *arrange* for one, confiscate one or more directly put, take one by means of force or guile. All the good intentions of the past had been shelved for the time being. Their first day away from the monastery saw them at their second day without food.

As both men had finally mounted their horses again and were ready to ride toward the southeast, it was the White Priest who suddenly began to laugh loudly. A strange look of shock overtook the facial expression of the Manchurian: one which seemed to ask for an explanation while equally showing obvious annoyance.

"You better take your sword off your back! We've returned to civilization, remember?" The White Priest continued laughing as he irked his friend on.

"Civilization! Is that what you call this dust bowl out here?" The Manchurian, aggravated, at the same time unshouldered his weapon in order to conceal it sideways under a wide leather strip, the hilt now barely showing. "I guess I better tie it down," said the Warrior. "If we have to gallop I'll definitely lose it." Pausing for a few seconds he then went on, "You better hide your weapon as well. Somebody told me that it's against the law for tribesmen to carry any weapons at all."

"Yes," answered his friend, "so I heard, but all the Mongols I've ever seen were armed to their teeth!"

During their conversation they had already started to slowly ride towards the southeast in the direction of the Munku-Sardyk which was somewhere on the tip of the Hovsgol Lake. The Munku-Sardyk Range rose up to a height of over three thousand meters and would aid them considerably as it towered over the rest of the landscape. The Hovsgol Lake stretched from here straight south, approximately a hundred and eighty kilometers in length, and at its smallest width a good sixteen kilometers from shore to shore. The lake was known to be stormy and unpleasant, cold with rocky cliffs and impenetrable mountainsides.

As their journey continued the vegetation became increasingly more luxuriant, larger spaces between the many millions of trees interspersed with dense birch coppices, oak and cedar. This, at times, made the ride easier and permitted the men to cross the countryside without relying on the main road to which both of them felt an understandable aversion. As the end of the day arrived and as they made camp and remained there for the rest of the night, the morning sun climbed to the right of the snow covered mountain in the distance. The third day had begun since their departure. Afraid of making a fire, they had not slept well. It was simply too cold. The hot month of July would drive the temperatures very high during the day but would permit them to slip dangerously toward the freezing point once darkness set in. The hour was far more advanced than when they had awoken the previous morning. Most of the game had already grazed and therefore disappeared again. The men prepared themselves and soon, without eating or drinking anything, they began to travel into the new day. It was not before long when the lead rider, who in this case was the White Priest, loudly and happily announced the finding of the great waters, as the Mongols referred to this particular lake.

"Fish, there are fish in the lake!" joyfully raising his hands the Manchurian exclaimed his thoughts to the rest of the world which in this case was here only represented by his friend.

"Wonderful!" echoed the voice through the expansive forest. "Just wonderful!" repeated the one whom the Manchurian had named Tiger. Although, a tiger would never really have a problem getting food: he was very capable of hunting and possessed still far more stamina than both men combining their strength and prowess together. One can easily adopt any name, however one can find it extremely difficult to bear in times when there is need and suffering. A tiger knows his medium: he can travel many miles without bother from fatigue or inclement weather or other such obstacles which would bring a man quickly to his knees. A tiger is also much more cautious than man. He would not storm downhill in order to welcome a change of situation as did the brothers when they were overcome by the powerful impression of a large, wide open space which, alike a fairyland, presented itself to the two adventurers. It was solely instinct that compelled the first rider to halt his horse sharply before stepping out and away from the cover of the huge forest. Only moments later his Warrior friend arrived as well, doubling his effort to stop his steed.

"Something wrong?" queried the husky rider.

"I don't know as yet but there could be," answered his companion while preparing to dismount, slipping quietly down from where he had sat. "Here, hold him for me. I'll take a look," and, passing the reins over to his friend, he left, walking carefully toward the water's edge.

The lake had receded considerably and a wide, rocky beach with long running, sandy streaks offered itself to the foreigner. Looking around and over the ground there was nothing visible which might forewarn him of danger. No indication of life was traced into the land whatsoever. As welcome as it must have been, it was also a sign of isolation: a desolate feeling which the empty stomach understood more than the searching eyes cared to admit. After a few minutes, the man on the beach began to wave toward his friend who immediately proceeded to move forward guiding the other horse along. Arriving at the spot where the White Priest stood, the Manchurian dismounted and left the horses tied to one another, standing by themselves. Drawing his Samurai sword, he walked away from his friend and over to the beach.

"Are you attacking the ocean?" called the one whom he had left behind. The White Priest was unable to observe his friend's cunning smile as he continued to step closer toward the spot where water and sand meet. There, a couple yards into the water, rested a large rock. Crossing a few steps through the cool waves, the Warrior placed himself on the stone, his eyes fixed upon the side where the shadow made it possible to see deep into the water.

27

Takuan was looking for fish. He had caught many of them in his childhood days at his grandfather's home on the ocean. But a sword was no harpoon! Takuan, burdened by such thoughts, gradually became angry with himself. A sword should be much better because it is swifter. Then again, he was unable to use it in the swordly manner, cutting and slashing at the target. Here, he must stab straight into the water remembering also that the image seen does not correctly represent the actual spot where the target, the fish, would be. There was this slight disparity which in all earnestness would make the difference between having breakfast or the continuation of a much longer and much hungrier day. The Manchurian having laid himself down, covered the entire surface of the large rock with his body, leaning over toward the shaded side. From this position he was able to see in detail a part of the lake: the flowing to and fro of the water played with the growth above the deep ground as if grooming the dark green strains which, floating with the current, began to reveal the structure of the bottom before it in turn would again carefully conceal everything which it had just uncovered. Takuan soon spotted many fish; but they were all small and too far from the reach of his sword. Then, suddenly, he was given a display of nature's own laws showing the hunter and the hunted. A large eel had caught its prey, a small fish whose blood began to discolour the greenish blue waters where it had been struck by the relentless jaws of the predator. Being preoccupied with its victim, the eel forgot about its own safety and the gleaming steel of the long sword, the sharp tip, penetrated the winding animal behind its head. As his catch surfaced in the struggle, it was not too difficult to apply the sword in its proper manner which was that of slashing at its prey. Cutting a half meter into the algid water, it did its cruel work separating the writhing hunter into almost equal parts. At the same moment, the body of the Warrior slid into the waves, his sword between his teeth now presenting a much less known picture of a once peaceful monk. He had no trouble catching both ends of the parts which seemed to struggle with each other. Freeing his hands, the Warrior quickly threw at first one end toward the shore and then the remaining piece; both of which landed far up on the moist, sandy beach. Swimming from where he was to the rim of the water took little effort. Wading out cold and wet, the Warrior removed his sword from between his teeth in order to give forth a triumphant yell - rather unbecoming of a man who had learned to control his emotions to an almost perfect degree. His friend, however, was conscious of the immediate result only and thus equally as happy. Long before the Manchurian was able to reach the land, he had secured the slower struggling portions of what appeared to be a huge meal.

Still out of breath, more from the excitement than actual work, Takuan announced, "You see, it was accomplished in the shadow of the rising sun!" while he raised his hands in the direction of the round disc as if all answers come by way of its light.

Hugging each other and jumping around in a circle, the friends had begun to share in a remarkable change. It was the first note toward a new life and it was also the beginning of the realization that they were able to survive away from the sheltered existence they had led for such a long time.

"I am the hunter," resumed the Japanese looking directly at his friend.

29

"- and?" questioned the other suspiciously.

"And you, of course, are the cook!"

"Well then, I have to know what to take out and what to leave inside, right?" Tiger had deliberately phrased his question with the intent of securing only one response.

"Just take out everything. That way you can't go wrong,"came the reply from a much more clever man than the younger one cared to admit.

"Right!" was his friend's only comment.

Now, in joy and joyful confusion, both of them ran about securing wood and arranging stones properly in order to shield the fire which was quickly set. Rapidly it began to bellow smoke up into the fresh morning air, fortunately drifting not over the surface of the lake but away from them. The huge trees swallowed all of it as if it were proper to keep the whereabouts of the two men hidden from the prying eyes of the world. Before long the steel pan, which constituted one of the more precious possessions of the two men, began to perform its task. The eel inside had been cut into small pieces and was browning on the portions which stuck closest to the hot surface. This cooking utensil had in fact belonged to the gear of the Mongols whose horses they had secured, together with whatever else they thought might assist them in their escape from Outer Mongolia.

The brethren decided to continue alongside the shore southward. With their first meal ended they now felt good; and, ready for their journey, filled with new hope, they continued on. At times, they would ride side by side and then they would exchange the lead, always careful to observe their surroundings.

The wider part of the lake's northern portion had the appearance of an ocean. It was not possible to see the east side of the lake other than the high, massive mountain which only partially revealed itself in the hazy, late morning air. The green and brown rising hill and the white mountaintops which assumed the shiny silvery blue colour of the sky seemed to mix at times. The quiet water reflected the light as it became brighter while the hours progressed into the day. They aimed directly south which, following the contours of the lake, would bring them sooner or later to the town of Hatgal. There, at the crossing, they would make the final decision as to whether they would change their plans according to what circumstances presented themselves.

Riding along for several hours their conversation finally ceased altogether. The warm sun had turned into a hot, relentless pursuer. The horses, which were not shoed, began to exhibit the first signs of displeasure for they had walked a considerable length of time over the rocky surface. By now the two men, thoughtful as they were, chose the way around such collections of rock and hard soil whenever possible. This worked well though they did not make the gains they had set out to achieve. After the sun had reached its highest peak on the firmament both men dismounted and began to walk alongside their horses. Having not stopped for several hours, they decided to rest through the hottest part of the day, withdrawing into the sheltering halls of the forest. The Manchurian proposed that his friend try to sleep first. Afterward, he too would take advantage of the great pause and ensure that his strength was replenished.

Gazing into the distance, across the lake, both men were

surrounded by an indescribable peace. Engulfed with the feeling of remoteness and abandonment, they at least could benefit from the awareness that they were safe. As the hours passed them by and as they had changed the roles of being a guard and being guarded, the time had now come for them to rise and move on. It was at this point that the one who was called Tiger by his friend spotted a dim smoke line above the horizon. By his pointing toward it, no explanation was needed.

The Japanese began to speak calmly, "Yes, I know. They are somewhere, many of them, thousands and millions of them!"

His friend was unable to guess his thoughts as to whether he was pleased with his observation or not. They had learned that the towns here could be extremely large like Ulaan Baator which was said to harbor close to two hundred thousand people within its immediate vicinity. This contrast wherein one could encounter totally desolate regions which suddenly produced clusters of concentrated masses of people was always present.

The main road curved alongside the east shore of the lake and surely all the traffic remained there as well. It led to Moeroen and then on to Ulaan Baator. They knew they had to rejoin civilization somehow but they also realized they must be careful and therefore had as yet not decided on the correct approach. As of now, it was only important to bring sufficient distance between them and the Sayan Range which they, by this time, had accomplished most admirably. It would still take them four full days to reach the southern tip of the lake. The uncertainty as to whether the beach would remain usable for their horses caused some uneasiness, but a *wait and see* attitude proved to be the best they could adopt - at

32

least for the time being. The men would ride, then intermittently walk beside their animals. Switching in this fashion, they were capable of sustaining a certain fixed speed while at the same time saving their horses' strength. The stops were more frequent as the day began to demonstrate its length, its duration. The longer growing shadows reminded the men to seek shelter for the night. After tending to the horses, permitting them to graze and rest, being well tied on longer leads, another night away from the hill commenced: one which would prove too short in order for them to recover fully.

As lucky as the day had been, it ended on a sad note. There was no further meal to be had. Though tempted to use their reserve ration they, however, decided against it and instead sought out rest. Feeling safe and unobserved, it was the first time that neither of the two stood guard. The horses, being accustomed to the wild, would alert them in the event that anything unforeseen should occur. And so it was - only that the horses provided a very late warning indeed!

Both men awoke confronted by a group of Mongols on horseback riding towards them. The sun had not as yet revealed itself other than in its attempt to colour the sky a strange pink which distinguished itself from the shading dark blue that still clung to the passing night. The young man was alerted first waking up the Warrior who had been far away, passing through a vast Nirvana in his mind. Awakening under the distinct pressure from the endless, aggravating nudges his friend gave him, he jumped to his feet ready to engage in battle. The Mongols, still thirty meters or more away, were not as yet alarmed and it took all the persuasion the Tiger was capable of to convince his friend first to wait and secondly to see!

33

Upon coming closer, it was the Mongols who, gesticulating, called out what appeared to be happy and excited sounds. Being close to an old oak tree, the White Priest noticed the Samurai sword of his friend which had fallen to the side of the resting place of Takuan. Having first grabbed it while jumping from where he lay, he had dropped it quickly following the brief exchange with his friend. Now it was visible and a source of danger. Fortunately, his young friend was able to hide it without any undue commotion. The blanket, being as yet spread over the ground, aided in the disappearing act. The obvious mannerism with which the nomads presented themselves indicated a more conciliatory intention on their part. They were smiling and had women in their party. Apparently, it was an uplifting event for them to find people where they least expected them to be.

The general historic observations as to the characteristics of the Mongols did not make sense thought the young White Priest to himself. Now, just when he had expected problems, it seemed to be the opposite. The lead rider of the group had in the meantime halved the distance sufficiently to permit both friends a better look. The group, approximately fifteen strong, hurried their horses suddenly as if they were unwilling to wait longer than necessary to examine the discovery they had made on this early morning. Up to this moment, they had shrouded themselves in silence, with the exception of the sounds they freely sent before them when they initially spotted the two travellers. The first rider was an older Mongol, his white teeth gleaming from beneath his large furry cap which sat diagonally across the entire curvature of his somewhat condensed but huge skull, the bristles of the fur sticking out from the rim, the longer ones protruding yet above the others which coloured themselves in different shades while the first counterglow from the sky highlighted them. *Truly a Genghis Khan of the twentieth century* thought the young man to himself, observing this complete person in front of him.

"Aawa Hovsgol Dalai," opened the Mongol with his greeting after which followed a barrage of words, puzzling both friends completely. Touching his chest with his right hand he, remaining on his horse, gave a sign of respect or greeting, bowing slightly to the strangers.

"What did he say?" questioned the Tiger his brother, speaking under his breath while at no time allowing his eyes to provide any indication to the older Mongol who had just spoken that he had not been understood.

"He's talking of the Father Lake," returned the Japanese his answer in the same manner, bowing slightly and with perfect grace back to the visitor.

The other riders began to close in surrounding the two men in a half circle. Keeping a good distance from the two, they brought their horses to a halt. Still dancing back and forth, some of the horses appeared not to find this confrontation as yet suitable. They acted as if the interruption had spoiled their plan to surge on, decreasing the distance they still had to travel before the hot sun would slow them down and force them to seek shelter. There were actually two women amongst the men. Contrary to tradition, they wore a semi modern attire. Their boots were laced, their jackets dark green with zippers and slanted pockets and dangling from their necks the women, each of them, carried a huge set of binoculars. The females had sidearms whereas the men, only a few of them, carried old rifles. The young White Priest detected a row of horses which were tied together. Laden as they were, neatly and correctly the straps fortified with counter straps, it was clear that they were being confronted with some type of expedition. Not understanding what it was all about, the Japanese decided to make the first move. Approaching the closest of the group, he offered his greeting to the still seated rider. Then, turning back to the rest as if to get verification from his entourage, the Mongol decided to do the same. Leaving his horse with a peculiarly executed maneuver, he lifted his far leg completely over the animal's neck and bounced onto the sandy ground. He then proceeded to hug the other man. The Japanese had not felt so much hardiness for a long time. The young women, as did the rest of the group, followed the example of their leader. Soon everyone had dismounted, the horses were led away to the nearby trees where some were secured and others just let loose to run about as they wished. Off the first horse someone removed several square cartons from which numerous utensils appeared. It looked as if cooking time had arrived! Truly a miraculous sight for the two brothers. Sure enough, several of the other riders had gone into the forest to gather wood. It was obvious: the breakfast was about to be prepared. Still the conversation was slow and cumbersome. The old Mongol wanted to know who they were. After a minute of difficult exchanges the friendly Mongol was satisfied.

"Our comrades here are going to Sinkiang," resounded a voice which would have won any of the British announcing championships: the ones which are traditionally held in order to find the most penetrating and furthest carrying human voice.

Both men were wishing they could cover their ears which, of course, would not have been too diplomatic faced with the present situation. Very little was as yet established. The two friends had certain reservations as to the authenticity of the group, for the events which had occurred only a few days ago were still fresh in their memories and thus left them doubtful and suspicious.

"What in heavens have you told him?" asked the younger friend of his Warrior companion as soon as the first opportunity presented itself.

In the meantime, everything else had assumed an attitude of daily casualness. The women introduced themselves from a distance while some of the followers of the group aimed for the denser part of the forest. It was a general time of rest, a pause which was held more, it appeared, because of the discovery the old man had made. They had been several days en route and had not encountered anybody at all during their journey. The girls were in their late twenties: one appeared to be Russian, while the other one bore the distinct characteristics of a Mongolian woman. She was younger and remained more distant from the new travellers preferring to busy herself with her horse. The excitement waned as each and every member of the group had certain chores to perform. Within this involuntary confusion, it had finally become possible for the two friends to exchange further conversation and as soon as the occasion permitted the White Priest repeated his question once again, asking what in heavens Takuan had told the old man.

"You see," answered his friend quietly, "I know Chinese and

37

you speak some Russian. So we are both a sort of remnant of a leftover army which doesn't exist any longer. I told him that we are on the way to Sinkiang province to volunteer for work there." Pausing momentarily, he quickly added, " - which I thought was the best answer considering the circumstances - and by the way, the old man was elated."

"It certainly would help if you would tell me as well. Don't you think you committed an error by talking Chinese to a Mongol?" asked his friend half naggingly.

"No! What does it matter? He answered in Chinese which makes my story, at least for the moment, more authentic. Actually, he can hardly speak it."

"Well, he sure answered you fast for a person who can't understand very well, don't you think?"

Takuan agreed but as the events began to lead on to other things no further discussion was wasted on the subject matter. The Mongols were of different tribes and some would not speak at all to the others unless necessity dictated. They looked as if they were hired to support the caravan for whatever purpose it was equipped. It would also be helpful to the brethren if they could learn the aim and destination of this group. But for the moment a wait and see attitude was again the best they could assume. Following a rather peculiar custom, only the one who had begun the conversation with a stranger bore the obligation, in due time, of introducing the acquaintances he had made to the rest of his kind. Therefore, both young men knew that the entire introduction had as yet not begun. However, all they really cared about at the moment was the meal that was being prepared and that, for all things in heaven, was something to look forward to! One remarkable trait commonly attributed to the Mongol is that he enjoys company and once a hugging has been given the law of hospitality is in force, as sure as the sun sets and rises out here. For the time being, therefore, both friends were safe and, much more so, they had found a group of people who enjoyed company as they, themselves, were also on a mission which had led them away from home across the wild countryside.

Amidst the increasing activity of the party beside the lake, it was the rising sun which began to lend the first tentative signs of hospitality to the group, mingling shadows and light, bodies and bushes, trees and rocks, tossing them around in a scene equipped to please the Almighty. There was no hostility rather there was a hurried laughter where caution had been first observed and somewhere the smoke began to nebulize the beach away from the searching eyes of the two friends who had been engulfed in the hustling and bustling as if they, themselves, were a part of the group. The efficiency with which the Mongolians worked was as swift and mind boggling as the scene itself. The quiet spot over which the two friends had just struggled in search of a destination had been turned into a busy campsite. Upon further examination both friends noticed that many more riders were armed than it actually appeared at the outset. Several fires began to flicker and light steel pans and pots being placed over them were slowly filled with delicious smelling food. Someone started to play a mouth organ which lost its soul as the rest of the party joined in to the tunes while still working, running, cooking, and performing all in all. It was as if the situation had been created for a play about the bygone days of the great Khan, barring the absence of the many different coloured tents which remained unpacked on the horses and the camels. It was a colourful party all right, a mixture of everything, the sun blessing so many different peoples, tall, small, brown, white and yellow, men and women and animals and a noise which had generated itself into a sound that could outdo a swarm of hornets.

Chapter III
Tsai-li

The arriving day was met with changing activity and changing trust amidst the people confronted by different cultures and, much more so, new attitudes wherein the ancient and the modern found mild conflict. The two travellers from Altan Tobchi had blended into the colourful scene which, fortunately in the end, prevailed over their differences. It was in the early afternoon when all fun was pushed aside. The leader of the expedition had set his mind to continuing on. As soon as the word was given the same assiduous activity began once again as it had occurred when they unloaded their animals in order to rest. The novelty over the strangers whom they had met had passed and the distant horizon, the descending sun within it, reminded them to not forget their goal which was to travel further west. The Manchurian had initiated an immediate relationship with the pretty Mongolian girl. Much laughter and much more information was exchanged between the two. It was learned that the group was destined to reach the far away regions of Sinkiang near the vicinity of the old town of Yarkant. It was practical for the two brothers to remain with the group if at all possible but in the overall context of the expedition's aims it was highly unlikely that the leader of the group would agree with such an amalgamation where the two brothers would simply become a part of them. Having outlined during their conversation with the Mongols that both men were

41

aiming in the same direction, a common interest was momentarily shared. But it remained to be seen whether it was advisable for the two to press for further considerations. For the time being it was practical to leave things as they were. During the market-like, adventurous activity of breaking up the camp it was the Mongolian girl who had chosen to exchange more words and interests with the Manchurian. As the time of parting was about to arrive, it was agreed that the two friends should follow the caravan and meet at their next resting place once more. It was also established that the Soviet girl was actually the leader of the troop. A geologist from the Moscow Institute of Geology, she was also schooled in party matters and followed a strict line, one specially outlined for the trip into China. The political struggle in Sinkiang as well as the other regions of China was still active. The younger generation, radical with less life experience, was storming head over heels into the accomplished revolution. With pockets of resistance still left in the eastern part of their country their overzealous drive had as yet not exerted itself sufficiently to have finally been exhausted to the point where more reason would be permitted to spread. The general situation was tense and a slight distrust by the Soviets of the Chinese could be felt. The Mongolians tended to side with the Soviets, having had little or no chance to meet with the counterpart to their Chinese brethren.

The shaggy horses of the two friends were soon rounded up. Being well nourished by now, they also were energized by the activity and the adventurous urge of the rest of the caravan. It was at this time that the Manchurian approached his friend. Having his sword still hidden beneath the blanket which willingly provided it shelter for the day, it was now his task to skillfully roll the blanket up with the weapon inside, carefully watching that it did not reveal itself. In all likelihood, no one would have noticed nor cared - but then, one could never be certain. As much as friendship was revered out here, suspicion was a greedy observer. The Asiatic courtesies were only too well observed making it doubly difficult to assess a situation.

His friend was informed that Miramsita, the Mongolian girl, would ride predominantly at the end of the caravan since she knew the two brethren had to take the same route as the main troop.

"She understands Japanese. One of her brothers chose to fight on our side in the early days of the conflict, but he got killed by the Chinese," explained the Manchurian. This information led to a new directive and all previous planning was now revised. Both men decided to stay apart from the main body and follow it at their own speed. Should a confrontation with unfriendly nomads occur, they would wait and observe first before participating. In any event, it was up to the brethren either to join the Mongols or to avoid them depending upon the situation.

Meanwhile, the girls began to wave and the old Mongol gave the sign to mount their animals. In a slow, locomotive movement the ball of man and beast began to unravel following the shore flowing into a dark line parallel to the quiet waters. A march of many days had begun before they would finally reach the southern city which they must bypass. It was generally expected that any traveller should be experienced enough to fend for himself and only then was it estimable if one group of people would join up with another one, neither becoming a burden to the other. Hence, the first discussion which transpired would assure the different sides that they were independent of one another, simply having a common route in mind thus benefitting from each other's company. Olga, the Soviet girl and likely the older of the women, had spoken with the scout, the elderly Mongolian man. Having travelled in this area for many years, he followed his experienced sense of direction with an unimaginable stoicism humming a forgotten tune of bygone days to himself, repeating its melody a million times over.

"What a delight not to follow him for too long," began the Manchurian the conversation once more with the White Tiger, a nickname for the White Priest used much more frequently now by his friend, the swordsman Takuan, who had rediscovered his human emotions. The girl was on his mind and no matter how much he tried to deceive himself, she remained there.

Not long after Takuan had struck up a more lengthy exchange of words with his friend, it became noticeable to the other brother from Altan Tobchi that a new lease on life with the rest of the world was being issued after the long hideaway in the Sayan Range. So it was fitting that, with some sarcasm, his friend began to answer, "Yes indeed, not at all a delight to follow the old Mongolian!"

Speaking thus, the White Tiger swung himself onto his furious looking horse and the Manchurian turned back as his eyes forgot to follow the fast disappearing girl who had promised to ride at the end of the caravan. But as clever as she was, she would not reveal her intention too readily to her companions. In a slow gallop, the Soviet expedition began to bring more and more distance between themselves and the two friends, the travellers whom they had first greeted with so much enthusiasm and from whom they now seemed to be hurrying away in contrast to the earlier hours showing that space and time - and ambition - could undo what the wonderful coincidence of good fortune had so quickly created only to be equally and as readily cast aside. But neither the Manchurian nor the Mongolian girl would accept this very simple trend without giving life another chance. And so it was understandable that the two brothers required little effort to stay on the heels of the caravan, close enough to not eat its dust but never too far to lose the shadows of its riders against the setting sun of the long day which did not dare settle from this unwarranted separation as yet.

The beginning night announced itself with an increasingly cold stream of air which touched on the disappearing ripples of the dreaming waters. Bedding down for the night had become one of the first routines both brethren had accepted since leaving the sheltered forest of Altan Tobchi. Being reintroduced to the world at large, the immediate struggle resumed with such a speed and vigor that many of the valued lessons ended up as good intentions only. The daily exercises, the many routine chores necessary to make the monastery function had removed them from more worldly things. Their hideaway, the monastery of a common fate, had brought together many different men where the need for brotherhood and most of all the fear of being discovered were sufficient deterrents such that they blindly obeyed all that which was outlined by the Abbot. In this way his leadership was never opposed. His wisdom breathed of suffering, experience of life and understanding, an untold sort of comprehension of each and every man's individual make-up. Now, being surrounded by this modern day continuation as it seemed, the ways of Altan Tobchi began to be altered rather dramatically. The young Mongolian girl had struck a dormant chord within the Manchurian. Being in hostile territory, governed by the urge to return to his people, he had already been sidetracked by his emotions. He spoke very little but exhibited a new drive towards life. Thus, he was reluctantly accepting the fact that it was indeed time to rest, for the new day had many things in store and somewhere in the distant future the two brethren must separate: one of them turning east while the other would attempt to go through Sinkiang and Kashmir into India - away from the territory of Soviet influence, the Stalinistic empire.

Now, since the night had finally made room for the newly arriving day both men proceeded south towards the larger city, still following the Soviet expedition with due care. Noticing their tracks, it was assumed that the Soviets had taken longer pauses and were not travelling as quick as anticipated, judging from the previously ambitious statements of the old Mongolian scout. Ambition and factual accomplishments are two different things especially here in Asia. After several more days of travelling both men arrived at the crossroads. Studying the ground the men noticed the expedition had turned away from the city road. Dust hovered over it and the covered sun seemed to hide itself from the earth as its subdued light played with the wrestling clouds of the dried out substance. Being on slightly lower terrain, they observed a convoy of trucks driving from west to east. It took several minutes before the last truck disappeared together with the swirling momentum the vacuum had created, sucking in huge clouds of dirt behind them. The Manchurian was shading his eyes from the bright white sky through which the sun finally reappeared, its blinding intensity impeding any further observation in the direction of the disturbance on the main road. Both the men's horses were stomping the ground with impatience, their hind quarters dancing sideways, swaying the riders back and forth as the scene continued.

"They've come from the west," verified the Manchurian in expectation of a reply. However, his friend was busy freeing his eyes from the white sun's glow which began to filter through the dashing low clouds of dust that by then had reached them.

"Yes, they are Chinese militia units I would imagine," answered finally the brother who, casually working on his saddle, began to measure the surroundings with increasing distrust. "Hatgal must be left of us," suggested the same voice maintaining the sparse conversation.

The Manchurian's hand reached out to his gear which was fastened loosely on the right side. His long sword had been hidden in such a way that the saddle blanket covered most of it quite well. However, that last extended trot had exposed a part of the weapon once more and it demanded his constant vigilance to *keep the blade concealed from unworthy eyes,* as the Manchurian would say. Their mood was, despite all, still well balanced and hopeful. It was mutually decided that it would be advisable to retreat a few kilometers from the road to find a spot for the night. Hatgal was a large town where continuous traffic produced exposure to too many people. Both friends had little experience with the public. Their linguistic skills were limited or considered by themselves to be actually non-existent. Primarily now the Russian language was in use. All large towns had educated the young ones in the language of the administrative power originating from Moscow. However, some new agreements had been made with the Mongolian leaders for the preservation of their mother tongue. The difficulty was knowing where this was being applied and how much of their Russian was accepted and by whom, for some of the main functionaries were Soviet citizens.

The night was both pleasant and uneventful, cold and boring. Their empty stomachs were in search of food and had problems finding rest. The wind was cool and getting downright cold as the night proceeded to envelop these two adventurers who were seeking a way out of an uncompromising situation. The Manchurian, the actual Japanese escapee, and the man who had come from Irkutsk to escape as well, had found shelter together in the Sayan Range. Both ran the extreme risk of being recaptured and sent to a much harsher confinement. At least the open plains, the hidden valleys of Outer Mongolia, the organized disorder and the multitude of languages would provide them better cover and an easier way to blend in with the population. It was decided they would follow the Soviet expedition possibly into China proper and then break away, separating to each on his own find a way back home. Without money, clothing and guidance all this seemed to be an impossible task. So the days were not really planned rather left to develop by way of chance. All the plans had to be altered anyhow in the event that problems arose. The general route was towards the west. The white Russian would try to get into India, Kashmir or Afghanistan while the other man would take his chance with fate altogether. It was impossible for a Japanese to turn east and surrender to the

Chinese: either the Kuomintang or the Maoists would make short work of him. He never divulged his plan by talking too much, but according to an old Buddhist tradition he would follow his Karma.

Long before the sunlight could mark the sky both brethren were up. A few dried fruits were eaten and the horses gathered for the continuation of their journey. Following instinctively the opposite of the dimly marked skyline, they headed west. The animals had no problem forcing their way through the dense bush though the slashing ends of the branches cut away at the riders, unable to see or sense their whiplike actions as they prodded west, step by step. The horses had done well, nourished by the food which they were able to find in abundance. Soon the trees became less dense. The underbrush disappeared almost totally and after a few more hours of riding they had traced alongside a hilly curvature a parallel line to the road beneath them. It was noticeably turning in a swinging curve many miles toward the southwest only then to continue due west where the sand was warmer, the sun hot and the dust would bite away at anything ignorant of the dangers of a late year encounter with the sparse and inhospitable land of Mongolia. Soon the hills were receding to the north being eventually reduced to a fine blue and brown line reminiscent of a moment where time in fact had stood still. The climbing sun had begun to encompass everything. The cold night had changed into a rapidly advancing day. Other groups of travellers could be seen on the distant road: the crushed rock, some asphalt patches and more, much more solidly ground gravel over which millions of carts must have passed since man had discovered this forgotten piece of real estate enhancing his vision of the possibility that more land and more people might be found elsewhere. Presumably treading on the path of men like Sven Hedin, who had in that same vicinity crossed with his expedition, measured and marked, signed and reported to the Western world, were these two brethren aiming into the distance be their horses still willing. Becoming a part of the brownish green impressions on the distant soil was the caravan which only days ago had paused on the chilly waters of the Dalai Hovsgol. The west lakeside road had been cumbersome for the travellers. From time to time they had to abandon the primitive road and let their horses swim around the rocky protrusions of the mountain who had as yet not given man time to carve a roadway into his flanks. While the two riders were reflecting on their past days, both men quietly dreaming yet subconsciously observing the winding road beneath, it was the Manchurian who finally broke the silence.

"I take it you have also spotted our friends down there?" But the Tiger was not yet ready to speak. Thus the Manchurian continued, "We're only a few hours behind them and should have no problem whatsoever catching up." Still his partner would not bother to utter a word and again it was the Manchurian who could not contain his research of time and occurrences as they had presented themselves. "I think we've been cast out of the peacefulness of heaven in order to blend into the shadowy world of man," began Takuan once more.

To this the younger man smilingly answered, "Everything we see altered on this earth is mainly through the work of man. Even the religions are his interpretations of a spiritual world of which he has no true evidence. We are motivated to believe: we are then inspired and follow. This quietness here is not of man nor is it of heaven either. It is the world of the in-between: the state in which we find ourselves pausing as we travel on, following our guide, the spiritual leader of the unknown master who has alone the key to compare what is and relate to what is not. To us everything seems to be just as we see it. There is no other way by which man can relate: a hand that touches, an eye that sees and a spirit which tries to hold onto all of this." Here he paused in his deliberations thinking for a few seconds before coming back to the question which his friend had actually posed and to which he, being a brother, as yet still had not responded. "Yes, the expedition is not far from us. We should catch up to them by nightfall." Adding these words the Seng Shi, the White Priest, had obliged the Manchurian who had already given his horse reason by way of nudging and pressing with his legs to march on, slowly descending across a scraggly meadow toward the general direction where the stretched out highway had left its tracks. Both men were now able to ride side by side. "Come to think of it," resumed the younger man, "have you ever wondered why the expedition would choose the poor highway, I mean the west side of the lake?" looking at his friend the question was rather well put, so well put in fact that the Japanese brought his animal to a sudden halt.

"They're not a government group at all! They could have easily taken the good route. Why would they drive all their pack horses through the treacherous waters?"

"I was just thinking that too, Takuan. It doesn't make much sense to me either."

Meanwhile the horses had continued to walk entirely on their own as if some force, some invisible urge, drove them onward.

51

The Soviets definitely had sent out scientific teams but why would they travel so simply, especially down here all the way to Sinkiang as this group had led them to believe? The Mongolian tribes felt much closer to the Chinese Reds than to the Soviet state. Some of the shaman believers had been telling stories emphasizing that the great revolution in China was to be different from that of the Soviets. Apparently the monasteries were not being bothered nor the people and that was very important. Even some Buddhist monks had spoken of a tolerant peasant leader who had received much help from the Buddhist establishments in the distant hills of the vast mountainous regions of Western China. But there were different factions within the religious movements of China proper at the time. Some of them spilled over into the northern region over which China really had no control. The rolling hills and the semi-desert land did not permit secure borders. One thing was a fact - both revolutions were Moscow made. However, the one in the south began developing its own motivation. Built entirely upon a very strong cohesive culture, it seemed to be only paying lip service to the masters in Red Square.

As their discussion continued they were eagerly trying to catch up to the columns of riders far ahead of them. Separated not only by space alone but by dense and dry dust, the two brethren from Altan Tobchi proceeded to engage in a more strenuous ride. In the far distance the road began to point upwards against a massive brown silhouette of mountainous splendour - an eery beauty, a frightening account of distance and isolation yet an incentive for any adventurer given the chance to reach out and conquer such land having only the unknown and unforeseen to offer. The food rations were already sparse and the water supply as well was dwindling. The month of August had still hot days but already bitterly cold nights in store. They must get ahead and strive to travel vigorously if they did not wish to be stranded here in this starved out region. The winters were known to be brutal and devastating with little or no shelter. They would have to reveal themselves to the authorities in order to seek cover from the freezing cold and pending starvation. The herdsmen and the nomads could erect their yurts and roll in, crawl together for warmth and comfort, draw from their stored food, free of such fears as starvation.

The two brethren had to press on to bring distance between themselves and the Soviet influence. After all, they had no papers to prove who they were: a person with no documentation was inevitably a hostile factor to the Reds. But as of now the real winter was still beyond the horizon and the belt of the Orion only visible in the early morning hours. Heading downhill, they passed through tall, dry grass and some green pastures which were being irrigated by modern wells. The powerlines were strung robustly but wildly in disarray across the grassland ending above several rough looking concrete rings under which the well was shielded by a wooden lid from the flying debris of the hillside's swift winds.

"Over there!" pointed the young friend to the nearest of these wells.

"Fantastic! The heavens are on our side my friend!" exclaimed the Japanese. "Our karma is with us after all!"

Loosening the reins both men let their horses find the way and sure enough they began to trot nervously toward the source from whence the scent had touched their nostrils. Water! It was miraculously wonderful to see these animals contain their urge to drink. Having arrived at the site, the riders proceeded to dismount. Reaching the huge wooden nailed lid both friends needed a combined effort to free the top from the deep drop over which it was placed. The Manchurian, leaning over its narrow rim, threw a tiny stone downwards only to wait for an agonizing length of time until it touched upon the surface of the water. "It's there all right!" he remarked. "More than thirty meters or so. The problem is we don't have a rope long enough to reach down that far."

"There's another one only three hundred meters away from here," prompted the White Tiger, the young man who had made a name for himself teaching that which had been entrusted to him by his master. And now, being separated from the mountain, riding through the vastness of a hostile surrounding, he began to ponder over all that had happened. Being short of water, yet still aiming into the never ending distance of the remote Asian highland of Outer Mongolia, he learned quickly that one had to accept the inevitable in order to plan ahead. Water was now important: the horses should have been watered on the previous day, but the time and place did not permit them to do so.

The Manchurian swung onto his horse quickly, almost wildly, and as soon as he was mounted the animal shot away, carrying its burden for another few hundred meters. Without hesitation the Tiger did likewise and soon two wild horses flew along the hillside kicking up the dried earth until it hung in clouds of dust behind them. Pulling hard on his reins the enthusiastic Takuan paraded his horse right up against the rim of the water hole. Being now able to see around the curvature of the hill, he noticed hundreds of sheep and a few riders busy tending the herd. A long, thin pipe stuck out from the side and a pumping sound sucking away pushed out clear water, emptying it into an old wooden barrel which overflowed forging a little creek engraving a silvery line downhill. His horse was just about to drink when the other rider arrived. Urgently pointing toward the herdsmen, both men hurriedly began to fill their canteens. Only then did they permit their horses to drink. It was rather poor horsemanship for a good rider thinks of his horse firstly; but out here things were different. It was, after all, imperative that they filled clean water into their reservoirs. The horses had a much better ability to digest impurities than the two brethren.

"Look!" interrupted Takuan his friend who had been busy soaking the flanks of his animal with cool water. "They're coming. They've separated from the sheep."

The saddle blanket was wet and the animal had white sweat rings where the girth from the saddle touched its belly. Taking a casual look, he noticed that the herdsmen were not just coming but galloping toward them. Takuan reached for his sword feeling the hilt which was covered by the blanket just to make sure it was still there.

"If they mean us harm we better make a stand right here and now. I would hate to be chased through the entire continent!"

"Let's at least mount," thus called out the Seng Shi, the White Priest, "and see what they want." The lead rider coming up on their right side was leaning, stretching, far over the head of his thundering horse. Mongols love excitement. This was something new, something that had not happened to them for sometime. A pair of riders were actually crossing their land!

"I'll take the first one!" announced the Warrior eagerly. "You block the route of the farthest of them and then we shall see." His shaven head had begun to show a considerable new growth of dark hair since their travels had by now left them many days away from Altan Tobchi. Without head cover the Manchurian almost looked like one of the Mongols himself. By now the first rider had come close but the noise of the pounding hoofs from all the galloping horses made it almost impossible for the Seng Shi to communicate with his friend.

"Hey, they don't have weapons! Look, they don't have any weapons, Takuan!" Calling thus, the young brother together with his wild gesticulations made his point. It was prudent to remain cautious though. By this time the first of the wild riders had brought his horse under instant control. Tearing around and ripping on his reins with vigor and violence he made his horse rise up and then, standing on its strong hind quarters supporting it well, the animal dropped finally but hesitantly onto his front legs to suddenly stand absolutely still.

"Khutukhtu uula.." and another swell of guttural words flew out of the mouth of the middle-aged man. He raised both arms in front of himself and clasped his hands.

"They are Buddhists!" exclaimed the Manchurian. "Apparently, the mountain belongs to their holy man," was all he was able to whisper under his breath. His friend had quickly understood. In the meantime the two other riders had arrived. However, their horses did not rush toward the two as the first had. It was a very strange moment. The riders also removed their round fur hats and stuck them into their belts - and now, they as well folded their hands, pressed them together and waited. Neither of the two friends were able to speak their dialect at all.

Then the Seng Shi began quietly to utter the words, "Tsai li." It was as if a miracle had occurred. The strange offensive praying gesture, the challenge in the swift approach, seemed to have found a solution. The Buddhist phrase meant *"I have taken my vows"* and was understood by almost any Buddhist and obviously even by these three mountain men. They waited a few more seconds, slowly looking over the horses of the two brethren, and then the first man offered a faint smile.

"Khutukhtu," he said while pointing to the others around him. "Uula Khutukhtu," again the first rider speaking more emphatically as he folded his hands together his head slightly bowed repeated these words several times over. The brethren knew only that a Khutukhtu was the most holy of the shamans in the region. Evidently the hill and the land belonged to the temple and it was not permitted to trample the grass where it was green. One of the riders pointed to the far side of the well.

"I think I understand. They want us to go on," began the Manchurian confidently, "but not to step on the greener portions of the land."

"Do you speak Russian?" The younger brother posed the question to one of the other Mongols.

"Who wishes to speak Russian out here brother? They have closed our temples so some of our tribes are moving south into China though very much against the will of our Russian friends, you know," replied one of the men.

57

"You know the words in Chinese," the third rider now spoke up, adding, "You are good people," very much to the relief of the two friends from the Sayan Range. "You see, we are soon going south as well. We are staying here only to wait for two more groups, like that one down there. They are going home to China. We are of the Tibetan clan and wish to leave. There is no law right now. They do not stop us. They think we are willing to fight for the revolution. We believe the Red Chinese have a better place for us than the Red Soviets." With these final words everything now began to make sense. The expedition that had passed them were actually men wanting to resettle in China.

"They told us quite a story, my friend!" began the Manchurian. "Those riders and the girls are fleeing from the Soviets. They are sneaking out of the region, though quite legally."

"I got that much myself!" answered the young Tiger. "What is their word for water? We have to ask them for water before they push us on our way," cautioned the White Priest his brother.

"Usan! Usan!" began the Japanese rider, pointing to his horse which he had stopped from drinking when the three wild Mongols had stormed across the steppe. Shaking his head the Mongol began to dismount. Leading Takuan's horse back to the trough, he petted the animal. He then removed the bit after which the horse once more began to enjoy that wonderful silvery wet, pulling the water in with long lasting draws as if it was the rarest of juices.

The situation was saved! As strange as the world seemed to be, there were always friends amidst the most hostile of regions especially when least expected as long as one did not lose faith in his fellow man altogether. Admittedly, at times this was difficult, but for the moment out here one could find five individuals overcoming their differences, reserving enough time in the beginning to at least give the other side a chance. Luckily the Manchurian had not drawn his sword when the first of the tribesmen stormed toward them ending his full gallop only at the very last moment. But then the two brethren had a tiny advantage for themselves. During their seclusion and during the observances and practices within the Wutang Shan, they had learned to listen to their inner feelings, the vibrations which they received from the opposite side; and it was mostly this knowledge which gave them the initial advantage providing an emotional balance, etching out a mysterious superiority which was built on a simple confidence coming from within the soul. *The sage never raises the sword to see its shadow!* Thus spoke Fu Yen the teacher and guide of the young master who had never been tested by the spirits but only by man and who again together with his companion was being harboured and shielded by a people they had never known other than in the dark memories of their past which spoke of trouble, bloodshed and distrust.

Chapter IV
The Parting

R e-joining the caravan was proving to be not all that easy. The five riders had persistently followed the distant shadows which had poised themselves against the sky. Finally now, concealed by the swaying veils of the never leaving dust, they felt sure they would catch up to them on the following day. It was with this conclusion that they decided to rest for the night. Presumably the caravan which was still moving ahead of them would soon do likewise. The nights were notorious for being cold and dry in this part of the world. The horses, despite their fabulous condition, needed to rest; especially when they had been driven hard, and the *"Soviets"* appeared to be in a hurry. It was a time, however, when a certain mood of uneasiness seemed to linger over the entire land. Some fighting factions of the revolutionary Red Chinese Army had been known to cross through this area. The Mongolian riders were gesticulating and stuttering in an attempt to make their newcomers understand this. The Manchurian had no special wish to get involved with revolutionaries of any kind, most of all not with Chinese ones. The Japanese occupation of China was as yet not forgotten and a lot of Chinese peasants did not really carry a friendly heart for the Japanese. Thus, as tired as they all were, the Manchurian took the first watch voluntarily. Every two hours the turn would shift to the next man and so on. It was fitting that the two brethren began the watch, the White Priest following the Manchurian and then finally the Mongolians taking their successive turns.

It was suddenly, in the very early hours of this damp and cold morning, that the Manchurian awoke. His eyes still stiff, momentarily lacking any agility, soon began very swiftly to pass over the scene while an astonishing grimace engraved his face, derailing all the features which only moments ago had conveyed the pleasant touch of a deep sleep.

"Seng Shi! Wake up!" sounded the surprised and loud voice of the Manchurian. "Everybody has left!"

Indeed the three Mongols had disappeared as if the ground had swallowed them up, silently and apparently with very little effort. For a moment the awakening young priest said nothing, his eyes beginning the same performance as the Manchurian's had just finished. Jumping to his feet while looking around, he quickly began to check their baggage.

"Everything is still here!" burst out of his first words both question and exclamation at one and the same time.

"Yes," answered his friend, "nothing seems to be missing."

Pausing a few seconds, it was the Seng Shi, the White Priest, who resumed the conversation. "Strange don't you think? At first they scare the daylights out of us, then they offer to accompany us and now they disappear into nowhere!"

Nodding, the Manchurian added calmly, "Well at least we still have everything including our horses. Imagine if they would have taken them along! So let's take the bad with the good." Some unpriestly like sounding words were exchanged. The men made their breakfast and began to saddle their horses soon after. The sun as yet had not dared show itself on the horizon, not even the slightest touch of the well known, dim, white, silky line was yet to be seen. The stars were still out as if they were in the deepest of night yet it was only a short while away from the breaking of another dawn in the vastness of Mongolia.

As shadows come and go with the light in essence do they vanish also into the dark: two homeless brothers saddled once more on their quest southwestward still avoiding the great transport road. Having left the Hovsgol Dalai behind them, the *Ocean* as the locals would refer to the mighty waters, both men had now turned away from it and with each horse's gait brought distance between the past and present to the future to come. Those who are able to concentrate and control the mind, who have removed the unessential worldly desires and whose purpose is to attain enlightenment, only they can truly be called in the purest Buddhist sense *homeless brothers*. So it was then fitting, being without a dwelling and searching forth into the old and the new world alike, that by coincidence they were doubly homeless and twice blessed.

Far removed from the European civilization and far apart from it, nature seemed to have a common interest in all of its realms no matter where they were to be found, the new sunrise being nothing special in comparison to the rest of the world. Arriving here it had already passed the eastern regions of this vast land and in contemplation only a few hours ago touched the shores of Japan, the homeland of the Manchurian. The days on Altan Tobchi were always filled with suspicion. No one knew when the Red Ones would appear and detect the hideaway, the old inaccessible buildings about which many untold stories circulated in the area. Even modern man, the new order which denounced all spiritual cradles, could not but fear the region where folklore was nourished by the sages' stories of lost hunters and secret holy men mingled in with a ghastly array of doomsday talk.

The two friends had long since made some effort to catch up with the party which a day ago in fact increased its distance between them. During the war the Soviets had built a new road straight south to Moeroen - new, meaning here that some large machine scraped a ten meter passageway around boulders and cliffs always seeking to remain above the lowest part of the landscape though never climbing much in elevation either. The result was that this highway could accommodate only vehicles which would respect its primitive condition, driving slow, leaving the dust as close to the ground as possible. The column of equipment which was moving eastward had left the southerly portion of the road now aiming into the harsh wilderness toward the Egiyn River. The primitive roadway was not even suitable for horses: its surface being uneven, hard, rocky and at times covered with loose gravel-like debris making the animals slide and slip about whenever the road began to rise steeply, only to then drop drastically causing much aggravation and loss of time.

Riding downward from an elevated slope both men soon saw two distinctly different dust vanes in the distance. The one aiming to the west could only resort from the party in which the Soviet girl travelled, while the other must have been a convoy of some sort with a special task to fulfill. The Egiyn River does not flow quietly as it seeks to enter the great lake and to travel it upstream, and thus to forge ahead by challenging this unknown pathway toward civilization would be much too troublesome. The three thousand meter range which was waiting for them harbored only a few remote settlements of no significant value. Actually, since the war had ended a sudden revival of activity had overtaken many of these ranges. Dozens of scientific expeditions were roaming about, all of whom, it was rumored, were trying to locate the ever elusive uranium. Since these expeditions were so numerous and, at times, diverse in their aims, one was well advised to stay clear of any of them. The Secret Police had an interest in their findings, placing agents within each and every more significant group which could promise any valuable geological find. Being confronted with all these possibilities both riders continued with their thoughts and from time to time by mere gesticulation avoided actual conversation with one another. Anyway, the pace was being set by the Manchurian and a forced ride, as such, makes for poor conversation. The horses were well rested and responded favorably. The green pasture on which they had time to graze began to slip away from view as the road curved downhill going anywhere but south. Soon the morning coolness would change with the climbing sun. It was now when the greatest distance was to be achieved. The up and down, left and right, the sliding and slipping went on, neither of the men relenting. Taking a glimpse of the surrounding area, they were faced with a rapidly changing landscape. Their road was finally aiming into the sun but then after a few hours began to turn to the opposite direction. It was at this point when the lead rider stopped his horse, leaving it with a swift dismount.

"Enough for awhile!" laughed the Manchurian at his friend who still had a few more strides to cover until he drew close. Leaving his horse likewise both men stretched and swayed their upper torsos before talking further. Takuan, staring at the face of the Seng Shi, burst into a hearty laugh.

His friend, by now acquiring new reason, with a slightly embarrassed tone of voice asked, "What can you possibly find so funny out here?"

"You should see your face!" replied the Manchurian. "Your face is the result of your following me too closely!" exclaimed Takuan pointing at the dirt which had actually caked onto the perspiring forehead of his friend.

"Well, you've been riding as if you wanted to catch yesterday one more time!" retorted the young priest.

Since they both halted, the horses were still excited and uneasy being brought from a good stride to such a sudden stop. Circling and dancing about, neighing and tugging, they made it impossible for the two men to arrive at any worthwhile conversation. It took a few more moments until their excitement subsided and the animals began to relax somewhat. Then it was the young Caucasian who took the initiative, pointing southwards.

"Another day or so of good riding and we should start turning west," elaborated the young man, hoping that his friend had temporarily forgotten his plan to try to reach the crossroads in order to make his way homeward.

Taking into account all the desires man generally holds for peace and prosperity one had to be aware in this part of the country of the many dangers lingering in the unknown. There was a sort of civil war going on around them. The nationalists, the Kuomintang, and the Red Chinese had lost their liking for one another since the Japanese had been defeated. It was back to the drawing board once more. New edicts were issued, marching orders of all kinds and most of all new directives, political ones which would classify the aims of the National Chinese under Chiang Kai Chek as being totally undesirable. Talk had it of exploiters siding with the west, the big capital, the money of which everybody had never enough. So it was termed to be simply evil. If most people have no money it must be bad, hence the rich man had to be on guard even if he had acquired his holdings through hard work. To the peasants it would not matter. It never mattered in any event but things were very different now. Someone knew how to remind them that there were people who indeed had more than others. This, in itself, was already sufficient - indeed, very bad for the poor soul who had achieved something honestly. The rights or wrongs are never accurately measured whenever unequals clash.

The two riders, amidst all this, had other more pressing problems. However, they inadvertently could not help but be drawn into this struggle for they must understand it if they wished to survive for sometime to come. The Soviet Union had sent many of its scientists into Mongolia and further south into China proper. The far eastern part of the country was never really appreciated by the Western Chinese. Towns like Yarkant were resting on the rim of the end of the world in those days. The Kuomintang were east and they had to be driven into the sea. Some Japanese prison camps were still being maintained by the Reds and National forces. Days before, they had observed movements of soldiers, ragged and all, high spirited nevertheless, driving, walking, riding toward the West. Cognizant of all this, the young priest mounted his horse again, acknowledging the fact that it was time to behave like a good Mongolian. With this action the Manchurian had been given an opening and quickly fell into the challenge.

"You're mounting your animal from the wrong side, my friend!" exclaimed Takuan, observing well the change in his partner.

"Not the wrong way Takuan, the Chinese, the right way out here. Remember this is China!"

Mounting his horse, Takuan smiled under the strain of his movement and whipped up into the saddle. "The Kuomintang have no horses left here. They're all running over to the Reds!"

"Well then," replied his friend, "it doesn't make any difference whether the left or the right throws us in jail, does it?"

The conversation ended momentarily as the Manchurian pointed south into the grey sky, "Smoke! You see it?"

Hesitating a second or two, searching in the general area where his friend was directing him, he acknowledged, "What do you think that could be?" while his eyes remained fixed upon the source of the smoke. Drifting to the west first then moving southward, it left a thin veil of haze over the far horizon cutting across the vaguely illuminated landscape: the unevenly lit countryside hiding its origin well.

"What we're looking at are troop movements," answered the Manchurian while his horse, tripping and dancing, began to circumscribe a large circle in front of the young priest. "I think that the United Front has ceased: it's definitely coming from the west. I bet the Kuomintang has given up to the Northern region the railway to the south." Bringing his horse under control, steadying it, the brother from Altan Tobchi, the Manchurian as they used to call him, shaded his eyes and continued, "Well, at least there's no shooting discernible as yet. I'm not sure how we should continue?" Leaving these words with his friend he turned away from the sky to face the young man in anticipation of an answer.

66

"I think the best idea is still to tag onto the team, the girl, the Soviets. Surely they would know about the troop movements. They were in radio communication."

"I guess it would be all right, but I don't really know. I suppose this means good-bye Japan!"

"Well, you realize it doesn't make much sense for you to continue to go east. You'll never make it with your accent. They'll pick it up as soon as you speak the first word as sure as an anteater picks one ant out of a thousand!"

For the moment both men remained silent digesting these thoughts, searching for a solution. Meanwhile precious time was passing them by and as they stood there, side by side mounted high on horseback, it was the young one who first pointed his horse south, leaving the road at the fork on the hill, aiming to the eastern part of China, many thousand kilometers away into the unknown, due east, lengthwise of the Tibetan border into an empty China. It was obvious that the Manchurian could easily pass for a Mongol, his features coming closer to the image which made them outstanding in comparison to the young brother. Having acquired a good tan and more so being covered with his sheepskin and his leathery fur Shagil, as they referred to this cap out here, the White Tiger came closer to resembling a Russian in this particular part of the world. Being so very young might also help, provided they could make his existence plausible to whoever they might encounter in the days to come. The horses were doing well and the tempo at which they pressed them onward was kept to an affordable speed: affordable, meaning easy going while always aware that time was indeed of the essence. Another day would quickly pass by without the two men having altered their position very much. Twenty kilometers out here could barely move a pencil mark on the map, not noticeable enough to see any gain whatsoever; in fact, the overwhelming vastness of the land, its hostile environment, the fear of the unknown was ever with them.

Chapter V
A Piece of Red Paper

During the period of the great struggle, the civil war which raged from the early months of 1946 until the year 1949, a lot of stories had been passed on and written much less factually than the events which actually transpired. The end of the Second World War brought many changes and even out here the world would never be the same again. Within the last days of the war the Soviets quickly declared war on Japan, something they had forgotten to do throughout the entire duration of the great patriotic battle. In any event, the Soviets seemed aware that Japan would not bother attacking them: some efficient secret agent saw to that. Thus the Red armies could be successfully withdrawn and placed to fight the Nazi intruders. In all truth one cannot really state that the Chinese Civil War had this certain duration, that of only lasting a little longer than three years. The imperial armies of the Japanese had carved out the silhouette of what was to occur. All Chinese had worked loyally together to wipe the imperialist forces from the face of China. Since the cowardly attack on the United States in Pearl Harbor, it was only a matter of time before the awesome strength of that industrial giant would force the imperialistic Japanese armies to either face extinction or surrender. Island after island was reconquered: Burma, Singapore, and the Phillippines lay in the path of the aggressive forces of the United States which had the willpower and the means to crush an empire which had forgotten that it, too, had been given natural borders. Once the Japanese threat had been removed from China, it would soon become a struggle of ideologies with all other priorities slowly fading away. Vast amounts of money given to the National Chinese armies were redirected into doubtful investments with the troops deprived and confused as to the goal which was to be achieved. It was at this point that the leader of the Red Chinese group, which in fact had been small in number in comparison to the National Chinese forces led by Chiang Kai Chek, found a new meaning for their fight. A united China was more important to them than frail promises and rewards which purportedly would rain down from heaven! The control of the Western powers, still remembered well by most of the Chinese populace, and the knowledge of Chiang Kai Chek's alliance with these forces caused them to choose the peasant guerilla corps. Since the deciding battles centered around the railway connection in the north and since a change of warfare occurred, the complacent National Chinese troops were convinced of a superiority which in fact was non-existent. The Red Chinese Army had changed from a franc-tireur assault to a proper strategic all-out attack, leaving the shelter of their mountains and pouring with great determination into the flanks of the unsuspecting Nationals. The leadership of the Kuomintang (Nationals) quickly secured their funds abroad and the will to resist dwindled into nothingness when the Soviet Union began to support the struggle with arms and military advisers for the Reds. The American observers had no real commitment in China and as much as they had hoped for a more secure, democratic Chinese government, it was not to be. The last

69

U.S. troops on mainland China removed themselves as they, in any event, had orders not to participate and their stationary presence was only a result of the aftermath of the Second World War, fighting the Japanese not the Chinese. The profound respect of the United States for China could be seen in their maintenance of a generally neutral position. If any backing of the National forces indeed occurred, and there was some massive backing of Chiang Kai Chek by the Americans, it was done by supporting them with funds and moderate weapon shipments. The better equipped National armies, however, were poorly led. The Soviet support in the ideological struggle proved to be more significant to the people who had nothing to lose, rather everything to gain.

In observance of all this, it was not difficult for the two friends in 1947 to organize themselves accordingly. Being amidst this struggle and being well centered between left and right, one could never know which of the fighting factions one would encounter. Since the night was drawing closer, the dark lines engraving themselves where the deeper shadows lay, already both men had brought a mighty distance between themselves and their past. The monastery was hardly ever mentioned any longer for it seemed not to count out here; but the ties one formed had a peculiar way of remaining. Neither of the men had a secure future to look forward to and as long as they still continued to be between the two fighting parties mortal danger was ever present. The Red Chinese were everywhere. It would be safest to penetrate the main front and then, hopefully, continue west; but with the ever changing lines they never really knew which side they would be facing the following morning. It was during the nights that the fronts altered, when changes were made by successfully surprising the other side.

"Let's call it a day, my friend," announced the young rider pulling the reins of his horse firmly as he looked back at his companion who seemed to have been waiting for this already a long time. He halted his animal so abruptly that it raised itself on its hindquarters momentarily neighing into the falling day. The rider used the position of the horse to slide off backwards and down, petting it and talking quietly to calm it. Noticing this, his friend also dismounted in order to seek out a secure resting place. Blankets and other gear were unbundled and removed and the horses, now tied to one another, soon quieted down.

"This was a hard day!" sighed the Manchurian. "We started out slowly and then ended by racing up and down the countryside!" In emphasis, he held his hindquarters showing the other man that he had had his fill and in all likelihood was sore to the bone.

His friend smilingly sympathized with his gesture only too well as he nodded adding, "Soon your saddle will get softer!"

"No, I don't think so, it's all shiny. I better hope that my rear gets harder! Those last twenty kilometers were tough!"

At this moment the younger of the two Altan Tobchi brethren touched his pants somewhat where the seat was wearing thin, "Yeah, I wonder about my slacks. They're beginning to tear already." Indeed, the harsher pace had taken its toll on their gear and they were only at the beginning of this journey which was destined to bring them halfway around the world. "All our good habits, our practicing has been left in the past," continued the White Priest. "We should stretch and do some of our exercises so we stay fit."

"Not me," scoffed the Manchurian, "I'm bushed and I'm lying down as soon as I devour this bread here!" Both men were only too happy to do this. Some dry grass was being pulled and soon a sparsely lit fire began to lift a thin stem of smoke above the spot from which they would not leave until benefitting from a well deserved rest. As things progressed they had time to chat and it was the Manchurian who began, "The girl and her party should actually be fairly close by, providing they took this route."

Still busy consuming his dried bread, the younger man nodded and confirmed, "By rights we should have passed them. Look - " At this time he took the metal spoon which he had held and began to carve the hard soil in order to describe their position. "We went straight south but they probably turned yesterday and rode slightly east to avoid the rough heights over which we must have gone without knowing it. See?"

The Oriental friend made an effort to grasp the diagram, saying nothing at first until he felt he understood. "We must have cut them off, I guess."

"Yes, sir, we must have, if my sense of direction isn't fooling me. It also depends on whether they were riding as wildly as we were."

The Manchurian was elated. His face lit up, "We sure did go faster than the wind, my friend, which leads me to believe that we are indeed ahead of them!"

"The last sound of gunfire came from the southeast," remarked the young one.

"We should try to find out who is who. I guess the best idea would be to try to get behind the Red lines while we're still far enough north of where the real action is."

Listening well to what the Manchurian said, the Tiger added his own conclusions. "Fine," cutting directly into Takuan's thoughts he continued, "but how do we know whether these are the lines of the Reds?" and pausing for only a moment since he seemed to have the Manchurian's attention, "We don't know anything about the Communist Chinese forces other than what we have previously heard - and that was very, very little!"

Being slightly preoccupied with the bedtime preparations, collecting earth and sand for the blankets which they raised over a pair of sticks like a tent, the Japanese monk stopped momentarily to comment, "Well from what I've heard the Communists are much better liked by the poor people, subsequently we must appear to be poor to them, if we find them."

"I'm certain that we don't want to be found by the one party which means," and with a slight pause the young man continued, "we should put ourselves into a position by which we can be introduced by someone, thus all suspicion of becoming hostile to the wrong side would be eliminated. We made a mistake. We should have stayed with Miramsita's group."

"The idea sounds good now," answered the Manchurian eagerly, "but at that point we most likely would have stood out by imposing ourselves upon them. The best thing to do is to have a good rest and then try to catch up with them. The second meeting might put us in a very different light. We should have a well thought out story before we meet them, however."

Ending thus, both men began to do all the things essential for a tolerable rest which they had more than deserved. As the words and sentences were passed to and fro they arrived at a common plan. They would rest and be ready at the earliest possible time. Then they would attend to the animals and assure themselves once more of their position before departing into the rising day, trying to be accurate in the choice of their direction. It was here where their planning should culminate in success. Both friends had changed the direction many times over and, speaking in generalities, it would not help at all to assume much, but it would prove extremely important that they remain quite studious in what they were about to do. Equipped with this knowledge, they went to sleep. The scraggly horses were busy with themselves, chewing away and then finally, awhile into the night, they as well lied down to recover from their long and cumbersome ride. It was known that these animals had an astonishing rate of recuperation from that sort of hardship.

Being alone and dead tired, the night passed much quicker for the two brethren. Since the first glimmer of sunlight had already lifted itself high above the landscape both men found themselves in a hurry. The breakfast was thrown together: they did not bother with a fire in order to warm some food as they usually did but rather cut chunks from the last bread they had, hoping to renew contact with the strangers, the ones who had received them so well and who, as necessity dictated, they must like for the time being. It was a good plan both men had. They would try to rejoin this group and once successful decide on their next move. Both had discussed their plans - they were both trying to get home. But out here, even the best plan is precarious for it depends upon so many unknown events. Yet, one can, in general, arrive at success if one has at least an idea as to how to proceed and what to say in order to qualify for the wish of destiny, whatever that should become. They had been taught that destiny would look out for them if they adhered to the spiritual guides who were given to them. At this moment, being high on horseback, these guides had little to say as the two riders blended into the morning scene of southern Mongolia: a Mongolia still far north but carried south by their moods which had been strengthened enough for them to pretend that they had done very well for themselves in the past days. Immediately after their fresh start they reviewed their entire story. They were to be brethren of a Mongolian shrine which had burned sometime ago: the one that the Mongolians had told them about when they watered their horses just recently.

Aiming south southwest, they left the road on which they were riding and cut across the vast grassland, browned by the sun and weathered by dryness: a drought which produced a tough type of grass which was lashing out against the pasterns of both striding animals, spraying the fresh dew up against the leather works of the saddle mountings. The lead horse, throwing the moisture as high as the throatlatch of the closely following horse, was splashing the rider with water and mud. An adjustment was soon made with both men riding side by side whenever possible. As the hours waned with the long ride, the sun reached its high point on the sky and both riders began to slow down. The lead rider, the Manchurian, pointed to the ground using the sign they had agreed upon to indicate the need to rest. Since both men swung off their horses with great bravado, both got a small surprise when they landed on the grassland. Having not spoken with each other for a lengthy time other than the odd exchange, they definitely made up for it now.

"You're still leaving your horse on the wrong side just like the Russians do!" chided the Manchurian. "Out here they mount and dismount from the right side, in case you choose to be forgetful!"

In slight disgust with himself, the young priest shook his head in disbelief, "I better smarten up right now or else!"

Takuan interrupting, added, " - or else we are both going to be found out!"

"I'll soon tie my right leg to the saddle so I can't leave it the wrong way. That'll teach me!"

However, it was crucial that they make the right impression on the people whom they must mingle with. It could make all the difference in the world - especially for the dark blond haired man who would stand out markedly amongst the rest of the Orientals. Ironically, as in all strange circumstances one might encounter, they had heard of a Mongolian tribe that had tall, blond haired people riding with them. Some said they had been captives of the once powerful Hun tribes who had brought them from the Black Sea back here to their mountains, used them as servants for sometime until they escaped; they then, however, continued to mingle with their own kind for after such a long time they felt and behaved like Mongols.

While both men were looking into the distance for signs of life and traffic, they were unable to secure any indication of activity whatsoever. "We'll have to soon find a hamlet or something. Our food supply is running low. We're eating raw and dried food as it is right now," complained the younger man pointing to his rather empty looking saddle bag.

"Never mind the food. My saddle is getting loose and I'm afraid the wetness will shrink the leather to a point where my horse will get sore."

His friend laughed, returning, "It certainly won't shrink that much. Come on, you're talking about minor tolerances here!" Both men walked around their horses, petting them off and on while talking to them. It seemed that these animals somehow understood their plight. At least they were well tempered and only on occasion would they neigh and give way to small spurts of energy or discontent.

As they began to consume some of their remaining food, dried fruit and dried barley, their efforts to chew were highly accentuated and their efforts to swallow even more difficult. Since there was no water and since all the water they had was being kept as a reserve it was to be an unbelievably dry and dismal meal. The chewing would continue until enough saliva accumulated in order to permit that famous downward motion.

"I've been trying to get it down already for the last ten minutes, " grumbled the young Tiger.

The Manchurian, observing his gestures, added good naturedly, "Do like the ducks, shove your head forward with a proper tilt in the neck and then backward - it might help."

"Nothing helps!" came the choked words. "It's so dry I can hear it cracking in my ears." Craning his neck as he had been instructed, he continued, "No, I better try a sip of water."

At this moment his friend came from around his horse where

he also had been trying to force this paper blue broth down. Swiftly, with determined steps, his deft hand pinned the bottle against the saddle strap where it sat ready to be liberated. "Don't! You better learn to save water while you have something to save. There will come a time when we might really need it."

Waving about his arms, the young one gave in, mumbling something indiscernible but not important anyway. A stuffed mouth and loquacity are grave opposites in themselves. So it was that the normal wordiness of the Tiger was silenced. During this quiet moment was it the younger man who made an erratic movement, his head jerking toward his far left from where he imagined he had heard a sound of life. "Quiet Takuan!" and with the use of the full first name of his friend he found instant cooperation.

The Manchurian was also now listening intently into the bright day. "It's horses neighing," applauded his joyfully excited voice, "they mustn't be too far away. In fact, I think they're quite close my friend."

But the White Priest was not too easily overcome and cautioned that one should be first on guard before trusting, alike their practice of the art where one was taught never to be certain about one's opponent. "Let's take the horses away and hide them in the trench over there," and pointing downward to the right, his brother monk acceded.

Strange how things change so quickly out here. The monk-like togetherness had completely altered its meaning. There were no prayer meetings held any longer as the times were pressing and showed little tolerance to the two wanderers seeking only to survive, to make their way out from under, away from their hopelessness toward some sort of future. They had decided that they would speak about a monastery in which they had served for sometime, that they were on their way to seek work, any work, since both men had no real vocation. In the temple their handiwork was multifarious: no document or paper was needed to qualify for work as long as it could be done with some responsibility and quality. But the world outside was very different. Meditation is time consuming and demands a certain calm and restful attitude by the person and an equally conducive surrounding. So it was that since both brethren had left, very few of the habitual rituals were performed by them any longer. The world, in its complexity and problems, demanded more functioning things to be done. Both brethren had to seek out a way home. This was not too easily achieved; after all, they were in a hostile land. The Japanese could not very well blend into the society of the Chinese who had suffered immensely from the occupational forces of the Japanese emperor. The young man who had escaped his imprisonment would be at once recognizable to the Chinese as being anything but one of their own. The question remained who then could he be other than a young Soviet travelling with some military advisers of whom the Russians had sent many thousand lately in order to ease the time problem of technological advancement. So, for the Chinese this would suffice but what of the Soviets themselves? The capability to speak the Russian language well enough was definitely not there, since time is needed to speak without accent. In situations where surprise lingers as frequently as in the unknown, life's past flashes across one's mind, clearly and succinctly, only to be yet quicker absorbed by what seems to be beneficial for one's continuance. As they held their horses by their sides both men began the waiting game.

"I definitely heard the neighing sound of horses," opened the young brother, "and it came from where you pointed to as well!"

The Manchurian nodded eagerly and nervously, while raising both hands upward to caution him to keep on listening and not interrupt the silence with idle talk. Both knew within themselves secretly that they hoped to rejoin the first party of a few days ago. It would mean many things. Till now, they had very little knowledge of the outside world since they had lived in seclusion in the temple. As life had gone its way out here, it was time to fit back into the stream and flow of events.

At this point, they had withdrawn their animals deep enough into the depression that no one else could easily spot them. This, in turn, unfortunately, did not permit either of the brethren to look out over the landscape for the vital information they required. Leaving the animals both tied to each other's saddles in the lowest part of the trench, they quickly climbed up the ridge to where they could observe the entire scene.

"They can't be too far from here," concluded the young brother as he attempted to calm his inner excitement.

"I know, I know all that!" replied the Warrior. "But where?" as he looked around for any sign of foreigners. "They must be just south of us. I think I can hear the clanging sound coming from pots and things," and pausing here for a moment, he began to look over his shoulder. "We're dealing with some sort of illusion. The sound seems to be bouncing backward from that rock over to our right," he paused, deep in thought, still looking, listening and trying to verify his findings.

In the meantime the Tiger caught on as well. Now following the gestures of his companion he was also trying to pinpoint the direction and the imaginary spot from where the sounds originated. And then - there - finally, they saw visible proof. Smoke! A lot of it! Both men seemed to have seen it at the very same moment: one trying to point while the other had already raised his arm in disbelief.

"Sound certainly travels strangely. I could have sworn they were south of us!" whispered the younger brother.

"Well, now we at least know where they are but we better do something soon and make sure our stories match. For this time we're not only trying to make contact with them but learn something from them as well. Surely they'll be able to tell us lots, regarding the conflict between the Nationals and the Peoples' Army." Thus ending, the Manchurian had made his greatest concern known to his young friend.

"I know," answered the Tiger, "it'll be crucial for our future. We must find out how everybody is functioning and where they are moving, in short, who's winning and who's losing!" Sitting back for a moment they rehearsed their stories to reaffirm that they made sense. The young brother was to have been adopted by the temple while the Manchurian had fled into Mongolia from the Japanese, seeking refuge in the temple.

"Remember, I am Korean," smiled the Manchurian back at his friend.

They agreed to let this newly found group make the initial inquiries and as soon as they detected a change in their guests, they would drop the subject matter and revert to more pleasing topics. However, that indeed required great skill, since a question which is felt by the other side as being evaded would only lead to many more problems and speculation. Of this, they were only too well aware. So all was set.

"For the last time, my friend, remember, out here you mount the animal from the other side!" and thus speaking the Manchurian flung himself onto his horse high and straight, as straight as he had ever sat, waiting for his brother to do likewise, his horse dancing around in a small circle, its hindquarters remaining on the same spot all the time. Both men now firmly in their saddles glanced briefly at one another and with the exchange of *"Good luck!"* they proceeded to ride with haste and excitement toward the spot from where the smoke arose.

Both riders, the Manchurian in the lead, flew across the few small elevations and around the little bluff which separated them from the smoke. As they drew closer they began to slow their animals to a trot and then to a canter, finally bringing the entire cavalry to a halt upon arriving at the ridge above the group of dismounted riders. The very instant the two appeared both men and women in the group began to scurry for their firearms. One more rapidly than the other produced a long barrelled rifle, another an odd looking pistol accompanied by the customary guttural sounds being exchanged amongst all, those sounds closely connected with fear and surprise.

"What do we do now?" exclaimed the Manchurian. "Let's get out of here fast!" He had already turned his horse in such a manner that he could depart immediately if he so desired. But his friend, later, a split second later, began instinctively to wave and immediately the so quickly aimed weapons lowered themselves just as quickly in disbelief.

"Aiwa.. Aiwa.. how are you?" came the exuberant greeting from the young rider who sensed it was important to enhance his first gestures which had apparently been successful already.

At this point the Manchurian continued turning his horse full circle, now talking with teeth gritted, "Okay, my brother, let's go down slow - real slow."

Now it was the younger rider who had taken the lead, carefully guiding his horse downward toward the bottom of the depression wherein the group was assembled. As they were making their way downhill both men carefully observed the antics of the people involved while at the same time trying to determine whether it was indeed the same group who had approached them just recently. As the times were, the vastness of this land does not bring riders together as easily and swiftly. Therefore, it was with great relief that the Manchurian recognized the Mongolian girl whose name he had not forgotten and which he called out loudly across the open area.

"Miramsita, it is only us. Don't shoot!"

Likewise from the other side though somewhat delayed, but when it came, it came swiftly and impulsively, "Come down, come down, for heaven sake!"

Upon drawing closer to the small crowd, it appeared that all was not really well. Both riders could now see that some wore bandages on their heads and others across their legs and arms. Finally, the two friends reached the girl, who had narrowed the distance between them. She was the first to greet them. "We were attacked by a group of Nationals, we believe," began the pretty girl as she reached out to aid the Manchurian from his horse. Though now dismounted the Manchurian still held her hand as he scrutinized the nearest member of the group, wrapped in crude white material, shirtlike with stained blood seeping through in spots all over the middle of his body. "That's from a sword. It's quite superficial," explained the girl, her voice still excited, the words bubbling out.

The younger brother had dismounted as well and could see that something must have gone seriously wrong. A few more persons began to separate from the group as if to welcome the two riders. An older Mongol tribesman explained to the young priest that he had lost his brother the scout who, as it soon was established, had just died in the camp. That was the reason the troop had to stop in order to tend to the more seriously wounded. Most of the men were now very relieved and everyone wanted to explain and know whether the two foreigners also had any encounters. That question being answered quickly to the negative seemed to make them happy that at least the two had been spared the experience they had undergone. A few young Mongolian riders made very grim faces as they brought the dead Mongolian out from a primitive, makeshift tent. The dead rider, probably in his early sixties, had been shot through his chest, his tunic soaked in blood. They had removed the grey tufted material at the point where the bullet had entered only to just as quickly cover it again.

"We have to leave him here," said the Soviet woman.

A few of the others took some short folding shovels in their

84

hands, methodically scraping away the soil which as yet was not too hard beneath its grass cover. They quickly dug a shallow grave into which the old man was placed then covered with soil. One of the Mongols lit a piece of red paper and mumbled a few words as the smoke travelled up into the sky. He then gathered some large rocks which he placed on top of the flat hill. Since there was no mound left to see, it would be doubtful that any living soul would ever discover the spot again. The stone on top meant very little as a marker or reminder, for the entire area was filled with large and small stones, thousands of them. Only these few, for the time being, were different: one could see that they had been moved from a nearby spot where the earth was still fresh and the concave depression revealed the previous place from where the stones had been taken. In some regions the Mongols leave their dead outside, placing them upon a bed of stones a few feet above the ground so the birds may get to the body. Since these regions south of the Sayan Range are void of timber and since the ground is hard, it has been proven to be the most reliable method to speed the passage of the dead one. As fast as the Mongols had dispensed with their comrade, did they equally as quickly leave to distribute his belongings amongst themselves, talking in their Khalkha dialect as they finalized some noteworthy arrangements amongst themselves.

This rapid encounter with life and death gave the brethren from Altan Tobchi a very different view of the moment. It was in fact a time dictated by survival alone. As all this occurred within the first few minutes of their arrival none of the people present had really spoken anything coherent other than short phrases passed between the ones immediately involved. Now, since they had finished the burial of one out of their midst, the normal flow of life returned. Both refugees from the Sayan Range huddled around the Mongolian girl in an attempt to get enough information in order to assess the immediate situation.

"We were approached by a group of riders just before dark last night," began the girl. "They seemed friendly enough, we thought," paused the Mongolian girl brushing her leathery hat backwards so her blue black hair unfolded in the dim sunlight. "They were waving about so we did the same. That's why everyone was so nervous when you rode in."

"Yes, we too were afraid, you can be sure of that!" Pausing here, before continuing, the Manchurian looked up into her face, "Having a dozen guns staring at us like that!"

"Well, we couldn't be sure, not after last night!" justified the woman.

At this point the young brother urged his friend to let the girl make her point so they could learn more of what had transpired. These people were obviously still in the area. "And then?" queried the young monk. "What happened after that?"

"It happened so quickly, nothing really changed at all. They kept coming toward us. Then suddenly they pulled some rifles from their sides and handguns and they just began to shoot. By then they were directly in the camp. We lost four of our people."

"How did you get away from them?" asked the Manchurian in shock.

"One of our riders, we call him Tsur," at this she pointed quickly to him then turned to continue, "mowed them down with his automatic gun." The Mongolian in question, noticing the girl had pointed him out, produced the Soviet pistol, a long type capable of holding many rounds, as if to add credence to the story which he assumed she had been telling. "He had it hidden under his loose tunic all along so they could not see it when they first entered."

"I see," sighed the Manchurian to himself. "He still hides it very well, doesn't he?"

In the meantime all the riders had assembled and they were trying to make sense of the confrontation as well as to find out how much the newcomers could tell them. To understand the many dialects of the different languages spoken in this region of Asia poses a monumental problem. Nothing ever succeeds by means of the spoken word unless it is between two Mongolians of the same tribe. Since this rarely, if ever, occurs as one travels through any region, a multitude of dialects and often totally different languages seem to collide. Some of the people here were trying out their Chinese dialects while a few remembered the Mongolian word for intruder as the Russian words mingled with the Mongolian sounds uttered. Many hand signs were given and it seemed that between them and the telegram style words stammered out, reason actually prevailed. Suddenly things made sense. The girl whom they referred to as Miramsita spoke a good Russian and even a better Chinese, though her Khalkha was rather poorly delivered. Soon everyone began to speculate about what had transpired. It was believed that a few cadres of Nationalists had left the far south and made their way up here. Now, eight months later, the Red Chinese had caught up with the splinter groups and, in an attempt to force their hand, succeeded in engaging them in armed confrontation. Such encounters only occurred in brief intervals. A few of the

Nationals were killed as they withdrew further north and thus closer to the Soviet hemisphere. Soon this would mean that they would be stalked and cornered by special forces which the Soviets had ready and waiting near Ulaan Baator. Unlike the others, the Mongolian girl did not believe that the Nationalist Chinese forces would be that far north of the battle lines. Thus she thought that perhaps a group of marauding bandits had made their play for supplies. Still, they did nothing other than to attack the camp, leave four of their own dead once they met with resistance and vanish in the same fashion in which they had appeared, into the vast nothingness of the great grassland.

Chapter VI

Hatgal

The two friends agreed with Miramsita. Nationalist forces would never get into these far northern regions; yet, sometime ago it was learned that the Red Brigades had cornered a fleeing troop, shooting all of them. Sadly enough, there was little friendship shown to one's own kind as soon as the political thought differed. Takuan was counting the remaining group and arrived at a total of ten including Miramsita. Being in disarray yet trying to organize a common thought the group loitered about, the horses at times grazing, while somewhere, somehow, all this had to arrive at some form of reason.

"We make twelve riders total. We have enough provisions to last us for a few days," began Takuan. "How about travelling together until we reach the Moeroen-Tsetserleg road south of here?"

Miramsita translated his words to the rest and it was obvious by their gestures that they welcomed the extra company. Unable to accomplish much more in this area, all riders began to fall into a row and slowly remove themselves downhill into a curved maze of back feeding loops: the road made in order to master the steep downhill grade. Takuan, the girl and the young Caucasian took their positions near the end of the line. It would be a long and demanding ride.

After countless interruptions and long periods of hauling one of the lead riders of the troop announced sighting the outskirts of

Hatgal. Four dusty days and cold, damp nights later they finally had an injection of hope. Hesitating as he turned in his saddle, the first rider pointed downhill and soon everybody knew that the strenuous effort had brought forth a result. At this time the column halted in its entirety since the lead rider loosened the reins on his horse. All the animals were tired and eager for any rest which came their way.

"All right," began the Manchurian exclaiming his thoughts of relief, "we've finally reached the waypoint south!" The past day he had been riding beside the Mongolian girl and had talked with much delight and enthusiasm with her, resting only when the road became too demanding for man and beast alike.

It was early afternoon when they all paused, looking at the brownish, dusty hamlet which presented a rather dismal picture in the dried out valley before them. A few of the horsemen proceeded to dismount and stretch their limbs until all of them, finally, left their saddles and began to mingle. The Mongolian girl, Miramsita, produced a map which provided a rather good detail of the entire region, side roads, dried riverbeds and all. The Caucasian and his friend quickly adjusted to the scene and joined the circle which cautiously began to form.

"This is the town here," explained the girl pointing on the map. "We have to decide whether we wish to go into the streets or avoid the hamlet altogether." Miramsita spoke with her eyebrows raised in concern. Placing the huge binoculars against her forehead, she viewed long and carefully the scene before her and announced finally that the streets seemed to show too much activity.

"Let me see," said the one rider whom they called Ling, reaching for the glasses of the girl who readily passed them across.

90

"There are trucks and many horses over and behind the bend, lots of them!" came the sonorous voice of the rugged man across to the rest of the group who were nervous, over-excited and yearning to rest. Takuan and his friend were concerned and as soon as the huge rider returned the glasses to the girl, Miramsita began to look for the second time, long and searchingly, verifying the finding of her teammate.

"Troops, about a few hundred or so!" she exclaimed.

"Bad news for us, my friend," interjected the Manchurian, addressing the girl who only seemed to hear a part of his concern as she reached the glasses over to Takuan.

"Have a good look," she said, "over to your right in front of the long shack - and there." Pointing to the left, she made certain that the young Manchurian would not miss a convoy of vehicles which were parked, camouflaged and all. It was obvious that the group had to make some serious decisions. The two friends were still unable to judge the purpose of the small caravan in which they had been travelling for the past days. They also misjudged the whereabouts of Hatgal and thought already a few days ago that they in fact were rather close to it. They learned in the meantime that this was not so. Down there, in the brown dry air of that afternoon, the lead rider made the identification of Hatgal. An arduous ride it had been and they were only at the very beginning of their journey. The Manchurian had to eventually decide as to the continuation of his trip: either going home, that would be east, or following destiny rather moving onward toward the west. One thing was for sure - the farther they moved west the better it would be for the Manchurian. It was suspected that the imminent military confrontation would

91

occur in the east. This accounted also for the troops moving eastward in great numbers leaving the cover of the mountains in the direction of the coastal regions, separating themselves from the slopes in an organized and systematic fashion. In observing all this, the Manchurian reminded himself that the Chinese had little liking for the Japanese and the Manchurian knew that his cover could be revealed easily enough if his care would slip further into neglect.

Ling, the burly character, began to address the rest of the group. "Let's make some sense of all this here. We need a plan, I mean something to go by. We're on the way to the Yarkant region and we have all the necessary documentation with us from the highest Chinese authority, the very top officials operating in this area, guaranteeing us safe passage there." Concluding so, all drew closer as if his speech was an invitation to assemble.

Trust derives out here from simple speech, from the revealing of problems and assumably also from trying to solve them. The Russian girl, Olga, had remained rather quiet for some time and it seemed as if she had relinquished her leading role. This was the observation both friends made in the early days of their encounter with the group, Olga having been previously found in the role of commander rather than being subordinate to the Chinese Mongolian Ling as she now appeared to be. But as events would show, Olga began to slowly assume her old position. Requesting the map from Miramsita, she took a good look at it and compared her visual assessment with the town's activity.

"We shall bypass the town and aim for the great bend about seventy kilometers southwest of here. There are some shallow passages this time of the year: the Egiyn does not flow as rough any

92

longer." Before anyone else was able to interject, Olga went on. "These local Chinese governments seem to have more powers than you think. They suddenly decide to claim war measure conditions and have nothing to fear later on: it's that simple. I suggest we stay clear of Hatgal and rest here for the remainder of the day. Maybe we'll send a few of you into town to look for supplies, matches, oils, rice flower and millet seed." The rest of the onlookers seemed to agree. They either were nodding in unison or showed affirmative interest, mumbling one word or another. The mood was set to act and it would not be long until the group began to discuss details. Who was going to go into town: who could speak the local language; and who would draw as little attention as possible. It was at once learned that neither of the girls should attempt this effort.

"A female rider with a well equipped horse and gear would attract attention," cautioned the Caucasian. Takuan agreed as well as a few others.

"We go then," addressed Tsur the husky Ling. "I speak local Chinese good. You speak coastal tongues, my friend."

"All right then," nodded Ling, "but we better leave the weapons here."

"Okay Ling ... but my knife, my knife goes where I go!" growled the Mongolian rider. The other agreed and thus they proceeded to plan their trip into town. They decided to wait a few hours in order to enter the streets with the onset of the night. "All cats look grey in the dark!" grinned Tsur at his comrades, obviously happy about his joke as he began organizing a resting place for himself and in so doing inadvertently gave the signal to bivouac, that it was time to slow down and enjoy some peace. As this occurred, both friends and the two girls got somehow close enough to each other to be able to talk more unobserved than before. The general mood was now more trusting since it was felt that the true opposition was waiting downhill in Hatgal.

Meanwhile Tsur and Ling huddled together and began to weigh their strategy as to how to approach the town, what to do and what to avoid at all costs. "Uncertainty holds strange properties within its confines," began Ling pointing towards Hatgal, over his shoulder, using his thumb in a lazy gesture. His partner nodded in agreement, his fingers groping backward to touch the well hidden large knife which was covered by his loosely tied tunic as if to verify the presence of the weapon. It was there all right.

"Look!" said the Caucasian, touching swiftly his friend who was still talking to one of the girls. "He has his knife shouldered on his back." The Manchurian saw how Tsur placed the wide bladed knife back from whence he drew it, reaching with his right hand backward across his left side past his neck, placing the blade into its holder without error. "He must be able to do that in his sleep.." laughed the White Priest, "because no one can be that accurate and swift without as much as a glance!"

Both girls had taken a liking to the two foreign riders so they talked and shared their observations together.

"The Reds are not much better than the others," Olga began, "but Mao forbade looting and mistreatment of the people. Food if it has to be confiscated must be accounted for," explained the Russian girl.

"And how do you account for food like eggs or chickens if you take them, especially in large quantities like his army has to?"

asked the Manchurian.

"Each soldier has a pocketful of tickets verifying Mao's promise. The secondary line either pays them or tries to make good for them," explained the girl.

"What a system," remarked the White Priest, "taking everything and then paying with worthless vouchers!"

Looking up at the young Caucasian the Soviet girl continued, "Well, on first observation this seems to be true, but the Nationals give nothing and also appear to feel nothing: this goes without saying. Mao's secondary troops are known to make good on vouchers whenever they have a surplus in their storage shelters. Trouble is these shelters are mostly empty and far, rather real far away. It was true that the dreaded Reds were keeping up a face saving operation," continued the girl " but, as feelings have it, it made a difference when the troops issued these papers, telling that they in essence felt sorry but such was the way of war. It never has feelings for the poor, anyway," and in stating this the Soviet girl stood up in order to take stock of the situation, the immediate surrounding as it were.

At this moment the Manchurian also rose to his feet. "You know Olga, from what I have heard this is true: the poor are not shown any feelings by the passing hordes, friend or foe. But I also saw even less feeling being shown to the few who had, by some misfortune, acquired some visible things, you know, goods like a piano or a violin. They trampled on the fiddle in the same way in which they smashed the Guarneri and condemned the people bitterly for being educated!" Ending with this thought the Manchurian began to mind his business addressing now only his friend in order to cover the many loose ends which they had not, as yet, tied up for themselves. Having paid no further attention to the Russian girl, both friends had removed themselves and were engaged in a vital assessment of their situation. At this time, totally unexpected, it was the Soviet girl who returned and was suddenly standing beside the two men.

"Mind if I sit down for a moment?" asked the woman while the brethren, caught within the surprise, showed no objection but were rather intrigued by the event.

"No, of course not," both speaking in unison made space for the girl and began to listen.

"It is your observation, if I am understanding your inference correctly, that war is not only hard on the poor, who have nothing to lose any longer anyway, but moreso on those who have just climbed the ladder to see the light," began the educated Soviet girl to relate to the previous comments of the Manchurian.

"Well, you see," answered Takuan, "that is my point: who judges what is in excess and what is not? Who in fact is rich; in short, if you have two bicycles and I have only one, you are the capitalist, right?"

"Yes, some people would make that judgement and that's what frightens me," replied the girl. "I have observed both of you," she continued, "and you do not really fit into the normal setting here. You are on your own and I am certain that you have no propusks, travel documents, right?"

The young men briefly glanced at each other and following their instinct relaxed their defenses. It appeared as if the Manchurian was going to answer her but when he scanned the eyes of his friend he at once left the answer to him. It came from the White Priest, fast, calmly and without the slightest hesitation. "We are more interested in the Chinese than in the Soviets, if's that what you want to hear?" concluded the young man.

"Listen to me," began the girl again. "I don't really care. I am enroute to Yarkant, they call it now Shache or whatever. We are still about a thousand kilometers or so away from Sogo Nur (lake). We have to avoid several main roads and most of all we have to travel the other 2500 kilometers by whatever means we can, by truck or train, camel or cart." Pausing here for a moment she continued, "Since there is most certainly no train we will try to use trucks if we can. I have wide ranging powers from the Chinese and Soviet governments. I can hire and fire, rent, borrow and ask Moscow for assistance. I say this only once, to make up your mind. I know people, and time is running short. Miramsita went to school with me in the Moscow Institute and lived with my family. We are out here to get away from Stalin's long arm. My parents and many of our loyal communist friends have all been arrested but they don't know of us. They never know of the rest and they never can do a complete sweep of everyone anyway. There would be nobody there to do the work, would there? Right now we need some more riders. We lost our people during the ambush and another one, who took off on his own. So what's it going to be?" ended the girl abruptly rising with great authority.

The young Caucasian caught the importance of her revelation; however, it must be that they were all at peril and Olga and Miramsita were the only ones who really knew what they were up to, the rest of the wild entourage had little capacity for planning

97

or anything pertaining to what their future would entail. A nomad comes from nowhere and also goes to nowhere. Their minds are more purposeful and direct: they deal with the day-to-day arrangements first, worrying foremost about the horses and food, the things which are of the greatest of importance out here. As the Soviet girl pressed for action and as she was leaving as quickly as she had come, she once more turned around only to sit back down with the two young men for the second time. Waving to Miramsita who had observed her visiting the young riders, Olga's gesture indicated she should join them. As Miramsita rose to oblige her, she bent forward to pick up a leather bag which she threw over her shoulder while approaching the three. The Manchurian, who had taken a liking to the Mongolian girl for sometime now, was visibly happy when he noticed her coming. Upon her arrival she quickly blended in with the rest, all of whom were seated near each other away from the crowd which had already accepted the routine of the evening.

"The government of the Soviet Union and the Chinese reciprocal authorities empowered me to hire these new riders here," laughed the Soviet girl. "I want you to make out their propusks Miramsita, use stamp and date but back date it so I can sign it under the Soviet administrator's seal. Leave enough room so it does not interfere with the Chinese chop, the square seal in the middle of the page! We are allowed new provisions in Luen or Ulaan Baator. We have been given first travel right out here and have a Chinese liaison officer to contact in Moscow in the event that things go wrong," explained the action motivated geologist.

Yes, Russia is large and the Czar is far, meaning here, that they all were more than an arm's length away from the great Moscow purge as it was in progress at this very moment. Soviet citizens would never talk easily in a group for fear of being denounced and it still took many days out here, being in the middle of nowhere, before Olga finally was certain that the two young riders had problems of their own. Miramsita had by now opened the large leather pouch and was fumbling amidst papers, pre-printed forms and pre-sealed documents in order to install the names of the two friends - each on their own document all that which was deemed to be valid in order to secure a safe passage. The two girls apparently had talked it over previously and the contact the Manchurian had made with the Mongolian girl was in all likelihood the one which allowed them to become official employees of the Soviet as well as the Chinese revolutionary governments alike. In a caprice of circumstance souls and events were being guided towards the essential human qualities, the like kind finding itself as if providence in fact is indeed a living force. The two women as well as both men busy with their *'paperwork'* and nearing the completion of it felt, for the first time, akin to each other. While the four were organizing themselves to withstand the eventuality of a suspicious road check, mainly conducted by the warring factions, it would be important, firsthand security demanding, to know which of the two factions were engaged in such inspections.

"We do have solid support from the Red governments," Olga was pointing to the documents and all the other paraphernalia she had placed in the leather bag Miramsita was actively guarding, still holding onto the crude leather support, a long sling, which, whenever she would shoulder it, allowed the case to rest on her side while being sturdily fastened at two points, one near her waistline and the second point of security being the loop carried overhead to the opposite side where the leather pouch rested. But right now the pouch was spread out in the pale sand amongst the four. Stamps and seals were all applied in order to equip the documents with a stunning presence of governmental authority, tied into a code system for which a portable radio would offer security lines, direct lines to the top movers and shakers of the two Communist systems.

"You," Miramsita pointed to Takuan, "should actually slowly become the carrier of the small portable sender. It only weighs about fifteen kilograms and needs someone who is capable of mounting and dismounting with great skill, that is quick like lightning."

"Dear comrade," answered Takuan at once, "they would not know that item to be a radio would they now and shoot at it?"

Miramsita, being seated flat on the uneven ground, raised one leg kneeling now on her left knee poised between getting up and staying down, looked long and caring at the pleasant Manchurian as she nodded in reply, "This radio is not known to be an item of contention for civilian minds. Yes, the military knows its shape and importance and has a paranoid suspicion linked to anything which could look like a device of communication." Pausing here for a few seconds she went on, "There are rectangular shapes and even round ones, long ones which are stored lengthwise beside the horse's saddle; but, all this means very little as long as you do not expose the antenna. It is drawn from its tube and extends out almost two meters and that's what they try to look for. So keep that wire in unless we have to send or receive, got it?"

100

"Boy, I see the light, clear and without shadow!" answered Takuan in a cooperative and very willing fashion, inserting trust and friendliness into the souls of the two women.

Around them time had prodded forward to the moment where the two riders, Ling and Tsur were going to *explore* the town of Hatgal. Both men were busy tightening the girths on their respective horses, which they had previously loosened to give their animals some comfort while they were grazing. Olga, Miramsita and a few other riders drew closer in order to overhear the details of the departure.

"Now then," began Olga, "show me your papers." Both men produced the thick brown envelopes, hammer and sickle laden. The Soviet girl nodded in the affirmative. "Where are your Chinese plates? You know, the wooden plates with the two square chops on them? Have you got them? They might be much more important so show them first," prompted Olga. Ling had found his Chinese identification at once but Tsur turned his pockets inside out growing more and more uneasy with every unproductive movement.

"No need, I speak to them!" began the nervous Mongolian rider.

"You don't have it, you don't go!" shouted Olga explaining that the Soviet propusk with the working tools of hammer and sickle were impressive, "but if these people down there are Nationals they will take offense to the cutlery. Crossing hammer and sickle in front of their eyes means certain arrest." As Olga was making her point the White Priest noticed the lacquered plate dangling from Tsur's neck, solidly supported by a waxed leather band.

"You have it on your chest, for goodness sake! Watch that you don't hang yourself on the strap," laughed the White Priest, pointing at the wooden piece which Tsur now grabbed, momentarily embarassed, but then producing the widest grin with the most perfect set of gleaming teeth in all of Mongolia.

"These are our passage past the gate of heaven. I sure hope they can read!" laughed Ling and rearing their horses both men departed their minds now set on their task.

They were going to enter the town from the side on which they camped so all could follow the event as it unfolded. The scraggly descendants of the Fergana, Przewalski horses - haired heads and bullish necks- in their hardiness did not seem to mind getting up and riding again. They carried their load with great strength despite the fact that their oversized riders seemed almost to be dragging their feet which dangled barely one meter above the rocky ground. Riding downhill made the animals more cautious than normal, loose debris rolling under their hoofs whenever they would place their weight wrongly. And so did they slowly but cautiously disappear, stride by stride, toward Hatgal. The rolling hills which were rising toward the west were now extending long shadows across the stony valley while the dim lights began to show themselves, randomly at first, but soon rather quicker, one jumping upon the next one, parallelling the disappearing sunlight. As the men rode into the distance their silhouettes merged with the surrounding dust and the fading daylight until only a brownish grey marked their positions.

With the diminishing daylight all riders extended their resting time and remained near their horses, talking while relaxing.

102

In such a way was it easier to wait for the news both horsemen would bring back from their exploratory trip. For the moment there was only time for speculation and they all were involved in the pro's and con's as to what would happen down there and what would not. Since they had all come closer to each other and as the discussion speculated with their destiny a somber mood had set in, fittingly so with the morbid surrounding. Here was a piece of land which seemed to be lost on earth: little greenery, the meadows, where they did show a few stretches of grassland, were more or less dull in colour, making it difficult for any poet to praise such a scene. It was in this setting that the waiting game began.

"It should not take longer than 45 minutes to get into town," speculated the Mongolian girl, addressing the two men and the Soviet woman who had remained together since they had organized the documents.

"In an hour or so it will get dark here," declared the White Priest. "Would it be smart to sort of light a small fire for them to get a better bearing in case they have to come back fast?"

Another rider, probably in his forties, overheard the words and answered from where he sat, which was only a few paces away from the group, "I doubt the Chinese will bother them. They probably won't even notice them, it getting dark and all."

With the ending of his words the expedition leader, the Soviet woman, began to speak very loudly obviously intending the larger group to overhear her, "My dear friend, you say the Chinese will not bother them? Well that all depends on which of the groups are presently down there. Remember, the Nationalists don't like the Reds and both, at one time did not like the Japanese. That's all over

103

now. Some remnants of the Manchurian army of Lin Biao are filtering south to reach the Kuomintang lines. We're better off with the Red Chinese army: they recognize the seals. The Nationalists, in case they are filtering through that town, better not see any Soviet or Chinese seal. If they do, they'll probably arrest our two men, being especially suspicious with the night falling in." By now Olga had gained the undivided attention of the people surrounding her and thus she continued, finalizing her thoughts, "Shanxi is Mao's zone then, south of the Yellow River in Shandong, the battle is uneven, the Reds holding the lines so the Kuomintang have difficulty supplying the Manchurian army which has begun to leave its mainstay and disperse south and west - and believe it or not we are somewhere here in the middle! So we better be real careful and maneuver with great caution or our documents and seals will be held against us. We should try to avoid Ulaan Baator, stay well west of it and interconnect to the other roads."

"That will take some serious consideration," began the Caucasian, by now as brown and wind burned as the rest. "Cutting across these ranges takes precise knowledge, better yet, real good topographic maps, and," continued the same person speaking, "certain foods, a good amount of grains and fat and the best furs around. I heard that in January the mercury near Ejin Qi can drop to minus 30 Celsius."

"Yes," nodded one of the Mongolian riders, "we know but we can overcome that. It's the horses. Horses can't feed themselves through the high snow. That's why we move hard and get south long before."

At this point Miramsita mentioned that if the Nationalists

were in fact in town they could never attempt to go east into Manchuria, since the route would lead them through a most difficult terrain, swamp land and few places to find food or to even replenish reliable water supplies. So the general consensus then became the hope that the Reds indeed were the only type of soldiers down there in Hatgal. Since this part of Mongolia was still, that is officially, protected by the Soviet Army, a nationalist Chinese group had to move quickly out and onward due south in order to find the remnants of their kind. The war was presently going very much in favour of the Kuomintang, the Nationalists, but the Red Chinese Army had engaged in major armed campaigns into unprotected Nationalist territory and had caught them lazing around, as one might say: relaxing on the glory of some fictitious victory.

As the time passed, all remained consumed with their own thoughts until someone else would again break the silence, speculating as to the severity of the expedition into town only to fall back into silence, waiting. Ling and Tsur had by now made their way down the shallow hill and were beginning to enjoy the level road as it presented itself suddenly, much to the delight of horses and riders alike. The perspective had now changed and the town of Hatgal actually appeared farther away since they had reached the level ground which should bring them to their target, the array of long flat warehouses, the ones they had previously seen clearly from higher up. There was no traffic on the road: it was still a secondary type, with washed away sections which had not seen any repair for several years. Even the horses kept a keen lookout. As soon as the road began to flatten both riders drew side by side talking and coordinating their plans as to their adventure to come.

"If they're Nationalists," pausing for but a few moments, Tsur re-arranged his thoughts, " I mean how'll we know they're Kuomintang?"

"Well we won't, but I know that they have a sun-like marking on their trucks, like a ring of flames, I think," answered the older looking Ling. He had pulled his shagil deeper into his face and told his friend to do likewise.

"If I spot such sun-like emblem staring at me, my horse and me, we're gone!" rumbled Tsur.

"Don't do that! If they do spot us you better keep riding, you hear? Only turn around if you can make it inconspicuous, then turn into some side street. I'll follow you. Only then do we turn around. You get it? We'll ride awhile in the other direction and then we can double back to our old route and pray they didn't make us."

"Yeah, all right Ling!" mumbled the man who was sloppily hanging from the top of his animal, ragged enough in appearance for anyone to wish him to pass. Tsur had left his side arm with the group and had only his huge knife along, a blade of steel at least a third of a meter in length fixed and mounted in a crude wooden handle. The long killer blade however was beginning to look through the primitive sheath, the stitches coming loose at the tip, barely carrying the weapon and as such offering little cover for the shining blade.

"Do something about your knife. The damn thing is sticking out!" prompted Ling while he was gesturing towards the weapon. His friend shrugged and pushed the lambskin over it as they began to approach the first shacks and a well lit building. "That looks like some government place," observed Ling, "they don't worry about the bill. There's still plenty of daylight without blasting away all that energy! Watch for any sign of identification," ordered Ling as they were riding slowly past the first dwellings of Hatgal. The well lit building proved to be an official sort of structure, more glass than walls. While both riders passed the place, they noticed uniformed personnel inside but were unable to identify much else. On the far side, in the shadow of the brightly lit area, someone had dropped a trailer of some sort which was raised and blocked but not connected to any tow vehicle. The people inside paid no heed to the men as they passed.

"We done good so far," uttered Tsur under his breath. Ling heard him without noticeably acknowledging the words his companion had just spoken. He kept his eyes and ears open and observed a group of people who were entering a house to their left side. It appeared that these people were not interested in the two horsemen either. Hatgal was about to be enveloped by the quickly incoming night, concealing the riders much more than before, giving them a dark grey cover which blended well into the scenery. They had by now left many huts and some houses behind them, their horses trotting as if they were on their final leg home. Tsur came closer with his horse to that of his friend, "Over there, look, trucks," his gruff voice cautioned. Ling saw them at once and slowed the pace in anticipation of a better view, buying time in order to situate themselves so that they could either turn away or keep on riding. It was to be the first confrontation with the unknown. They decided to view the trucks and barely hesitated when they saw them, behaving exactly as they had previously agreed upon. No sudden motions, no turning away, just riding

107

along alike two men who had made it home late from the desert. "See, red flag on the horse cart, there!" began the Mongolian.

"Don't point!" whispered Ling. "Just tell me where."

"Okay, okay!" grumbled Tsur. "D'you see the three, big, covered trucks?"

"I can't see anything!" replied the other man exasperated. "Not on the street. You mean in the driveway there, beside the funny house, the long shaped, flat one?"

"There - a flagpole - some sort of long thing," uttered the Mongolian impatiently.

" Oh yeah, I see! On the back of the last trucks there," said Ling. "It looks like they're Mao's men," continued the latter. "But I can't see the upper corner of the flag, can you?" questioned Ling his friend, waiting for his verification. "The reds have a big yellow star with some smaller ones closer to it," explained Ling relying upon Tsur who rode on his right, a few steps closer to the object than he himself was.

"I can't see. I see a white circle or something in the top corner," answered Tsur impatiently.

"They must be Kuomintang!" reasoned Ling. "Anything round is not good, for certain not!" At this point they were convinced that they were in unsafe company and were about ready to make their way to the left, then put as much distance between themselves and the trucks as possible by hiding away in the maze of side streets which began to branch out everywhere. Thus swinging to the very left, crossing over from the far right side of the street, both horses began to change direction moving towards the mouth of a dirt street which should soon conceal the ensemble. "I didn't see any people there at all Tsur, did you?" whispered the other man, desperately trying to assure himself that they had made the right decision. They exchanged several more sentences as they rode on removing themselves from the immediate area of danger. As Ling looked backward over his right shoulder he could not help but notice that some activity had begun in the vicinity near the parking zone, directly behind the huge trucks. The last one, the one which boasted the national Chinese marking, had turned its headlights on and was moving away from the site. It swung wildly backward out of the driveway, lurched to a stop and then it did what he was hoping it would not do - it chose the same direction the riders had taken. "Keep moving. Don't look back!" whispered Ling harshly to the Mongolian. In a few moments the truck passed the men without taking much notice of them. However, as it left the riders behind Tsur, who was closest, caught sight of a red Chinese flag painted on its right fender. He announced his findings as soon as the bright lights had passed them.

"Must be Red Chinese. Probably picking up war bounty from the Soviet Commander here," Tsur offered, his voice calmer now.

"You're right. It didn't make sense that the Nationalist forces would be in this town any longer. It's too far from the action," concluded Ling as he halted his animal. "Let's turn around and go further into town. We might be lucky to find some government supply store still open!" said the older Ling, his mood now optimistic as both riders made an about face turn, heading back into Hatgal. As soon as they arrived at the road from which they had just turned away more traffic appeared. This time directly confronting them, a group of military cars and several open trucks, displayed clearly the Soviet markings, a red star with a white outline, the latest exhibition on any new armor made east of the Ural Mountains. The column passed them, their headlights glaring as darkness had now totally taken over from the transitory twilight time. Both riders went on, confidence renewed, penetrating deeper into the town. By now the street was flanked with many buildings, some newer than others but all the same, all in a dismal state of repair.

Hatgal, just a year ago, saw General Pliev with his Soviet Mongolian cavalry, aiming straight south to Peking, there linking up with the Chinese Peoples' Eighth Army. Before and at about the same time Yamada's Kwantung Forces were being encircled by the Soviet Far East Army, its Thirty-fifth Army Corps, in addition to the First, Fifth and Twenty-fifth Army, the Fifteenth Army Group, the Second Far East Front under Purkayev and Maliknovki's Trans Balkan Front. It was, however, Pliev's march across the Gobi Desert which remains a little known feat of triumph in military organization and allowed for a swift defeat of the indecisively led Japanese forces. An area of more than 1,500,000 square kilometers was conquered in 24 days, an area larger than Germany, France and Southern Europe combined, a campaign which made Hitler's Blitzkrieg look like a horse and buggy operation. The concerns that Nationalist Forces could be found anywhere was more one driven by paranoia; yet, defeated splinter groups from National Kuomintang operations were known to be in action everywhere. In part there was a peaceful cooperation between the Reds and the

Nationals until the Kwantung forces were ousted from Manchuria. That cooperation would quickly fade into hostilities as the Nationalists lost the favour of the people, plagued by corruption and insensitive decision making.

In the wake of the occurrences of the past sixteen months both riders knew that some uncertainty would remain with them. Information from the newspaper and radio was only available to the government. The people in general did not know the latest changes, be they economical or military ones. Mongolia had its own currency however. The Soviet Military and services connected to political enforcement used vouchers and special privileges which were only obtainable through higher officials. Being well equipped with documents and tickets they could afford to engage in any activity which had to do with buying items, equipping their caravan and providing for directional aid. In short: anything extraordinary which was not covered by the military was covered under political enforcement. The caravan which was being sent to Yarkant was a political adventure and political favours always superseded military ones.

"Let's try that government store, there," began Ling, pointing out the place of his interest. By simply nodding, the Mongolian signalled his cooperation.

An uncouth looking crowd was gathering inside. The huge glass window allowed easy observation by the two men. As they approached the store, the horses turned slightly sideways until they faced the front of the structure. Both men dismounted and tied the horses to each other, a common habit out here. They would remain with each other until their occupants would return. Both men entered the store but attracted little attention. Fortunately, most of the people inside were busy with their own activities. The two outsiders took a glimpse around and noticed quite a number of military personnel. The walls inside were burdened with huge, primitive shelving. Some of the arrangements were faulty and leaning towards the aisle, laden with goods. One had to be cautious removing anything from the structure for fear that the entire thing would come along. Ling and Tsur observed this and had no desire to create any extra attention. They carefully removed bags of grain, sugar and matches, cases of them. In the hills they would find remnants of wood and debris sufficient to make a fire. Matches were a rarity out here and thus in demand. Since the store had a large supply of them, they took advantage of it and secured all they were allowed to buy. After spending barely twenty minutes in the store they were ready to leave. They had a chance to observe the composition of the population and concluded that the town seemed to mainly be occupied by Soviet controlled Mongolian troops and some military contingents of Chinese troops, who did not appear to have any special equipment other than their rifles. It was interesting for Ling and Tsur to discover that side arms were only worn by Chinese officers. They were of Soviet origin and Ling thought that they were the newer type, the automatic Tokarev version replacing the old 1895 Nagant model. Paying for the goods presented no problems. The men produced their tickets, a type of voucher which was mainly used by accredited officials; hence, little opposition was encountered. Leaving the premises, the horses stood ready and willing to make the return trip. All was well: the animals were burdened with the newly acquired goods and once they were

112

secured properly both riders mounted their horses and turned away from the store. Soon the dark night would envelop animals and men alike as they began to make their way back.

In the meantime Takuan, his friend and all the other newly made acquaintances huddled together, waiting for the *'scouts'* to return. Much speculation was being voiced and much concern being raised by the entire group worrying, hoping that all would turn out well for the two men who had the courage to ride into Hatgal. Takuan had indeed found a new friend in Miramsita as he exclusively spent time near her. Both beings had a liking for each other and it was as if destiny had interfered with purpose. However, the friends from Altan Tobchi had to be careful not to be discovered; after all, they had escaped from captivity and they were outcasts of a system which had little sympathy or feelings for those who were in the disgrace of their political order. His Caucasian friend began to be concerned about the relationship which was developing between Takuan and the girl for he felt it was becoming too obvious and others would soon notice. At the first opportune moment, the Tiger, the young White Priest, began to voice his fears as he spoke carefully to the Manchurian.

"I'm happy that you two get along as well as you do, but.." Rising now from where he had been seated he remarked that Miramsita was under Soviet government contract and that two things should be remembered: firstly, a good close contact was serving them well; but that, secondly, such contact could offer complications if others would observe or fear that an alliance was developing between them for they, as yet, were still newcomers. Waving his arms in a calming gesture toward his friend, the

113

Manchurian assured him that all was fine and that he had already thought of this as well. "I know..I know, Takuan," said the White Priest, "we now have first class documentation belonging to a bonafide Soviet government expedition and as long as our hiring is not challenged we should be better off than before." Both friends knew that a challenge of this nature out here was highly unlikely though, just the same, the arm of the ever watchful KGB could be found in the remotest spot. It was common knowledge that most post office employees who served the public had an affiliation with that special government force. Conductors and church officials as well were known to be on the payroll of the dreaded Secret Police. Therefore, any contact with any member in the group should be well observed and made with the greatest of care and caution. Since both friends had moments of privacy, they began to remind themselves of these facts and of the fact that they were thousands of kilometers away from home: the Manchurian trying to get back to the National Chinese lines and the Caucasian hoping to surrender to the British in India if he could make the *short dash* from Yarkant through the high mountain passes. The short dash would still involve a five hundred kilometer stretch to the Kunjirab Dabhan pass, finally leaving the territory in which the long arm of the KGB could still create serious personal problems. However, the KGB would rarely ever challenge documents which were issued by their own departments, subsidiary offices which could be found at almost any level of Soviet administration. As things presently were, it was smarter to live by day-to-day arrangements than to think of the future which would be tallied in the achievement of overcoming thousands of kilometers of travel - a journey which, right now,

114

appeared to be impossible to finish.

The group decided to light a small fire since nightfall brought crisp, cold winds coming dangerously close to the frost level. With the passing of the hours everyone up here had made themselves comfortable. The majority were attracted by the small fire which soon raised the fleeing embers to follow the updraft. It was a romantic setting carrying with it the flare of the adventurous. After all: two comrades were still missing. Miramsita returned to the side of Takuan, who in turn was resting close beside his brother from Altan Tobchi, talking, laughing a little, anything to help pass the time. The girl had covered herself with the proverbial lamb jacket which seemed to be the trademark of a true Mongolian, coupled with the cap, the shagil, which had three major flaps traditionally worn upwards: be it then that the temperatures invoked a different action, meaning that they would then be turned downward offering extremely beneficial comfort in the most inhospitable weather conditions.

"I feel very good about the news that you are both accompanying us to the end of our journey," said the Mongolian girl. "I think that Olga has a rendezvous in Kumul. There we will be linking up with a group of scientists, a large Chinese contingent with several hundred Soviet trucks and cranes. Kumul has the only major landing strip for jet aircraft," ended the pleasant sounding voice of Miramsita.

"How far is that from where we are right now?" wanted the Caucasian to know.

"Ah - let me have a look at my map here." At that moment she began to turn her leather bag around which was resting flap downward in the sand. She quickly produced an array of topographical maps which were all neatly folded following the sequential numbers from each previous map. "We are here," began the girl, pointing to the lines revealing the hill on which they had made there bivouac. "We will follow the Egiyn for another eighty kilometers and as soon as it turns directly east we shall know that we are about 40 kilometers north of Moeroen; from here we go east southeast for a long time until we reach Luen, close to Ulaan Baator. We must avoid it until we know its status and cut rather south again, crossing two major roads leading from the west into Ulaan Baator. Over here," she pointed now to a spot far south of that town, "we have arranged that a convoy from Baator will intercept us on the Bayanhongor road, to the southwest, see?" came the voice addressing the two men who observed with the greatest of attention what the map revealed.

Such precise maps were rarely ever issued and it should prove once again to the brethren from the monastery that these people seemed to be heaven sent. With their new documentation they were in fact living beings again and even more important, they had become an integral part of the system. They had, by the grace of the great power and by providence as well, a new lease on a future: a future of course always alluding to life. It appeared that the hostile world out here forged the different peoples together, either by instinct or simply by the knowledge that one would be well advised to have friends in this type of wilderness before one would seek out confrontation. Everybody in their group was amiable: Mongolia was a land which offered the harshest of conditions, from heat and lack of water to bitterly cold highlands

116

which would channel the arctic air over the dried up Gobi regions, offering either 44 degrees heat or 50 below freezing - depending upon the time of the year. With the year entering the fall season, the winter could readily invite itself unannounced: meaning that weather was almost impossible to forecast out here. The US had maintained a weather station in the Gobi region to aid its allies but abandoned that service just after 1945.

As the three continued to look at the map much more discussion ensued. It was held in a rather low key, voice wise; for, it was not normal practice for leaders of such a convoy to reveal very much to the hired personnel. They would brief their followers from time to time and this only when they were near a given point. The mentality of the herdsmen suited this regimen. They were never truly interested in anything which was weeks ahead. A week's travel out here could produce many changes: snow, rain, sandstorms and brutal heat capable of scorching the green grass to a pale grey looking straw. Aside from this, man and animal were challenged to the utmost of their capabilities. Many a horse would never endure a five thousand kilometer trek: not even the dromedary offered a guarantee as compared to the raw endurance of the rough and wily horses of Mongolia. Only a few dromedaries had been introduced to these far northern regions and some Mongols preferred them because of their ability to travel with a much faster speed than the Bactrian camel is capable of sustaining. However, it was learned that the Bactrian camel grows better winter fur and by being somewhat slower than the dromedary, it has proven to have a much higher rate of endurance and thus makes up for the imaginary speed with which the dromedary is being

117

credited. Unfortunately, both types of animal will make any rider easily seasick. This seems to derive from the peculiar movements both species, the dromedary as well as the Bactrian camel, share in common. Unlike the forward movement of a horse, the camel uses both legs on the same side in unison as it advances. It thus creates a pitching motion for the rider being on top, alike a falling and rising wave would, shifting and heaving all at the very same time.

Miramsita and the two brethren were still studying the map when Olga came by. "I am sure that you will not get the whole trip in perspective. We have to make several detours and, by the way, they are long detours. I wish we could avoid them but - since not all the Nationalist troops have been accounted for - we are expecting surprises," stated the pleasant looking Soviet girl. The first dim light of a half moon reflected across her face as she smiled for a moment, but then, with a rather grim gesture, began to point towards Hatgal. As she sat down beside the three riders, Takuan, his friend and Miramsita, she offered a faint smile. "I have been told that some Red Chinese soldiers also went on their own, preferring to remain in some forgotten valleys they passed on their long march." As Olga gave this information to the rest she crossed her legs in a Burmese position and began as well to take an interest in the discussions of the three, listening first when the Caucasian resumed, rather cautiously from where they had been interrupted.

"Since you have made us a part of your group," began the White Priest hesitantly, "were we both..." at this time the Caucasian motioned towards his friend, "sort of quietly listening to what you have been saying. You are going to skirt Ulaan Baator for certain reasons and are instead proceeding due south of it. As you will be aiming southeast in the beginning you then will have to reverse your direction toward the west. In fact, you will have to cover, on your first attempt, an uninhabited area of about 120 kilometers, crossing a range of about two thousand meters, connecting to Onjuul, the main road running north of the hamlet." The Soviet girl was listening with great intensity and as the man talking began to look at her, he slowed down as if his deliberations were meeting with disapproval from the young Soviet scientist.

"Go on, go on!" encouraged Olga who noticed his apprehension had begun to hamper their discourse.

"Are you sure that you wish to hear why we are wondering about the choice of your journey?" placed the young man his thoughts carefully across, seeking further verification from the woman who seemed to exert a quiet control over the expedition.

"By all means, go on!" urged the Soviet girl. She removed her dark fur cap as if it would aid her in absorbing the simple observations coming from a person she had just met a short while ago.

"All right then," the young man continued, "from Dalangdzadgad on we will have to cross a plateau which reaches an altitude of over 2000 meters, the main passages lying around the 1000 meter level. I understand that, according to fears voiced by some of your riders, marauding Nationalists as well as Red Chinese troops have turned into self-serving hordes. If this is the case, they certainly will not be found near main roads but will have sought out inhospitable areas, such as you have chosen!"

At this point the Soviet girl became assertive. "You are wrong. I have been ordered to take the outlined route as I marked

119

it. We are expected to meet with a certain party near Ejin Qi, about forty kilometers south of the lake, Sogo Nur."

"I see," answered the young Caucasian who quickly began to adapt to the words of the woman. "This of course changes everything. I had no way of knowing this," came his embarassed answer.

"No, no, do not worry about that. I, too, have been thinking and talking with Miramsita for sometime about the possibility that we are in fact being directed straight into a potential confrontation with marauding troops," began the girl to reply to the thoughts of the White Priest. "We are not certain who is waiting for us in Ejin Qi. It sounded as if a Chinese party was to arrive from the Suzhou airport and intercept us there.." explained the girl saying that it was extremely difficult to maintain a workable timetable knowing of all the uncertainties with which the journey might be burdened.

It was now Takuan who interjected and in his calm and quiet way suggested that the radio could be used to address such problems as long as a reason could be found by which the administrative branch overseeing the expedition some eleven thousand kilometers away could be convinced. The road from Moeroen west to Manhan would practically cut their planned route by half. The Manchurian was pointing to the crossing from Manhan to Hujirt: the map showed an old trade route ominously dotted almost as if to discourage anyone who was pragmatic enough to see the advantage of engaging themselves in such a daring adventure.

"We could follow the Ulungur River from Hujirt onward to

120

the south," added Takuan to his suggestion, "cutting from Bulgan across to Ertai. North from here at Koktokai your map shows another jet airstrip. The party which had to fly to Suzhou could continue on to that destination in less than three hours," exclaimed Takuan.

"Providing that we can sell someone back home on the idea, correct Comrade?" answered the positive sounding Soviet woman. They quickly learned that the distance to Ertai was around eight hundred kilometers. It was then that the Soviet girl and Miramsita pulled the huge map over to where they were seated, away from the newcomers. Takuan foresaw the intent of the Soviet girl and at once relinquished the charts. The topographical maps were arranged in orderly layers, folded inside to be pulled out in accordance with use.

Since the light began to glare into the night as the group looked upon the maps, Olga intervened: "We better lessen the fire and keep it controlled until we are certain as to what has happened in Hatgal. They should be back sometime during the night. Meanwhile, I guess we should all try to get some rest!"

The dark hours advanced far past the halfway mark of the night. Sudden cold winds swept downhill and became icy. Most of the group had by now secured themselves in their Soviet Army sleeping bags which were handed out to everyone. They would prove invaluable as the time marched on toward the morning.

Chapter VII
The R-5

Ling and Tsur were happily making their way back to the camp. Under the added weight their horses were less happy, especially when the uphill portion of the road began to make itself known. Both riders said precious little to each other, each of the horsemen attending to their animal, moving along while at the same time watching over the boundaries of the road. It dropped sharply to their left, as much as a hundred meters at times, sharing the deep dark night with the luring danger of the abyss. As the trotting horses began to labour uphill, they also began to move their heads more noticeably, breathing loudly and abruptly. Their nostrils noisily pressing the content of their lungs into the open as their muzzles vibrated in unison; thus labouring along, shouldering riders and freight with great tenacity but still with the loyal obedience which had turned the horses into most valuable companions, too often taken for granted and only appreciated when danger lurked and the rider's life and limb began to rely upon their performance.

Tesio, a lover of horses, observed the intelligence of the horse many years ago saying: in the confrontation with man, the horse feels the same sensation that the barbarian must have felt when conquered by the Romans, enslaved, and used as forced labor. To indicate to the horse that he must halt, man pulls on the iron between his lips and his teeth; to turn to the right, he pulls to the right and turning left he pulls to the opposite direction, all the while the horse enduring the pain of this rather harshly transmitted command. This is the vocabulary man has invented to communicate with the horse: despite the fact that this same animal can, by himself, without anyone taking the trouble to explain to him what is meant, interpret the various sounds of the human voice!

These two Mongolian horses were, however, loved and well treated by their riders. Both horses looked alike, having each a hairy head, being of the same medium height and carrying almost the same markings near the fetlocks. The fact that they were both black, sharing a shiny noir-like brushed coat, allowed the night to cover them so well that only the riders were visible with their white, lambskin lapels. Whenever the turns became abrupt the horses had to follow each other. They would toss their heads about as they attacked the short steep grades until they found room and a more level surface to relax. The town began to disappear and with the distance already separating them peace returned with the assurance that all fear of trouble now lay behind them. They were much more relaxed and in a state of joy, eager to relate their findings to the rest of their companions. As they drew closer to the camp the men began to feel comfortable about speaking again. It was Tsur who resumed the talk.

"Well, guess we made it!" said Tsur, the relief noticeable in his voice.

"You think we're that close Comrade?" replied the other man continuing, "I had some fast heartbeats down there for awhile, but everything went all right. We mustn't look too wild as yet!"

123

"You, maybe not," boasted the other man, " but I sure look like a raider!" Thus smiling while thinking of their common accomplishment both men continued toward their campsite.

Proceeding along at a moderate pace, it was the lead rider Tsur who first caught a glimpse of a campfire. "See, over there, Ling!" said Tsur, pointing at the same time into the direction of the flickering fire.

"One more bend from here," cautioned Ling. "That's the tough one!" the same man once more reminding his friend that they were not home yet while beginning to climb the last, steep grade. It was important that the men would not lose the caution to which they had adhered all along. The drop to the left side was substantial in height and the road support, the bank of the path, was unreliable. Any wrongly placed weight of these animals could make the soft sand slip away, taking horse and rider alike into oblivion. "We better stay more to our right, Tsur," cautioned Ling. "There's a steep rising turn in front of us, see!" Tsur was looking into the blackness of the night, the clouds having covered the sky since, making it both difficult and hazardous. But these men knew their land and had learned to not only well observe the present signs of nature but also to heed its messages, which all too often were rather obscure and could be misinterpreted easily by an inexperienced party. The desert presented dry sand with an even looking surface; yet, at times, it would also hide the perilous stretches of quicksand, offering a confrontation with a most deadly and heinous trap, perilous and torturous to any form of life.

Tsur pointed towards his left side where the remnants of a structure raised itself against the grey sky. The other rider nodded

124

as he had a quick look at this monument which both riders made sure to pass within a safe distance.

"It looks as if they got out," remarked the Chinese man, "the thill is gone but the rest is still there!" It was the work of that ever so elusive type of quagmire which can be bottomless and, out here, often encountered at high altitudes. It seemed that the wagon had remained in it since only a part of the front portion protruded as if to warn any *"passers-by"* not to infringe here. Soon both riders noticed that the road was beginning to rise sharply, entering the last stretch uphill back to where they had started from.

Upon their return everyone left their resting place and soon both riders were being surrounded by a happy, excited and very inquisitive crowd. Many questions were being posed at the very same time, not permitting them to answer any with clarity until the Russian girl began to push away the surrounding bodies which burdened the riders as they were trying to dismount. The goods which they had tied to their saddles were being cared for and the bags which were just resting across the saddles were pulled clear. The riders embraced several well wishers as they walked closer to the remnants of the campfire which was now barely holding its own. Takuan began to revive it by stoking the glowing embers and as the updraft proceeded to catch the bare matter, the fanning air revived the fire in a miraculous fashion, sparks and ashes twirling up from the ground to raise themselves high above the excited crowd of chattering human beings. After a few minutes the nervously probing questions died into silence while the Chinese rider proceeded to answer a question placed by the Soviet girl.

"We've sufficient supplies to travel on for another week,"

replied Ling. The Soviet woman had inquired as to the amount of food they were able to get. Since the clear night had changed into a cloudy mass in the meantime, the cold biting winds had also changed for the better, aiding the reviving flames in sharing more heat with the onlookers. With very little of the night left, it was decided to make the best of the remaining time by getting a much deserved rest, for the two scouts as well as for the others in the entourage. Soon all were huddled as close to the fire as space would allow, couples and friends staying near to their kind and, with the excitement ebbing, a new silence once more spread over the barren hillside.

Cold rain began to sweep over the hill announcing the first sign of the approaching day, as the wetted leather goods, saddle and gear, threw a dull impression across to the rising people. It was cold, the fire exhausted and the crew busy, readying themselves for a meeting before their departure. The Soviet girl and her Mongolian friend were with Takuan and the white Russian. On the far side of the hill a few riders sported a primitive tent: rectangular in shape, a canvas strung across over four light metal posts, the front two of them lower, where the rain ran down dripping in streams, soaking the entrance to it.

The Soviet girl pointed to the site, "Let us try to go out of the rain and meet inside there!" Everyone rose, following her with their gear. It made sense to have a meeting and decide which route to take from here on, looking at the maps for verification preferably in the comfort of a dry tent before having them damaged by the rain. Stomping through the many small puddles, the group of four made their way, heads bending forward.

126

"Oh boy!" began the White Priest following Takuan who, remaining closely behind Miramsita and the Soviet girl, was braving the sweeping rain.

The Mongolian girl, upon reaching the tent, spoke briefly with one of the men who seemed to have left the structure in order to begin to dismantle it. "Can we use your place to review our maps?" asked the Mongolian woman of the man who had started to carry his belongings from the tent to where his horse was waiting.

"Help yourself!" roared his answer much to the relief of all concerned. As soon as they were inside, they brushed the rain off their clothing then proceeded to arrange table and chairs in order to have a final conference regarding all their previous ideas. It was certainly a good idea to re-think everything since the rainy weather could easily turn into snow whenever they were forced to cross the higher elevations. Timing and caution were to be the guiding forces behind their thoughts. In a moment's time they had turned the three chairs, which were as yet not packed, close to the table which was composed out of several carrying cases harbouring seismic instruments. The makeshift table was rather low and awkward so all four decided to raise it by placing more boxes on top until the height was comfortable enough to allow them to view the maps while being seated. As the Soviet girl began to open the large leather case in which the maps were neatly arranged, all but the White Priest had seated themselves, leaving him to kneel with one knee on a straw mat observing the unfolding and placing of the chart. Orientating the map towards the north, Olga began to point to their location.

"We are due west of Hatgal. Here," asserted the Soviet girl.

"We must follow the Egiyn River south and cross the narrows there, then move slightly southwest to Moeroen." Everyone looked on the map and noticed the high mountain range in the distance, the dark colouring indicating a steep rise of the terrain on the southeasterly side.

"That means we'll have to pass through an area which climbs up to three kilometers," began the White Priest the verbal exchange which would follow as all of the persons realized the difficult journey they would be confronted with.

The Mongolian girl stretched across from where she sat suggesting that perhaps they ought to stay clear of the range altogether and follow the river only to the spot where it makes a sharp 90 degree turn to the east. "If we could remain clear of that range and not follow the valley where the river divides the mountain, I think we would be better off!" ended her emphatically spoken words.

Everyone agreed. They knew that they would have to cross a raised plateau which offered a ceaseless climbing and falling landscape. There were a few small creeks some of which were still expected to hold water and Olga pointed to four of them, three were denoted by dotted lines, meaning they could be dry toward the end of the year. Having just replenished their supplies to some extent and having a good deal of water with them, all looked well. Olga folded the map and announced that the four should ride at the front, only changing from time to time, appointing one to check the entire column. So it was agreed and as quickly as they all had entered the tent did they leave, more confident now as to what their plans entailed. The distance which they had to overcome to reach

128

the point where the river bends east was about sixty-five kilometers. They hoped to be able to cover this in three to four days. In the meantime, during this brief conference, the rest of the entourage had almost finished their preparations in order to ride again. Some were already seated high in their saddles while others were still wrestling with their gear as they heaved it across the backs of the eager horses. The entire caravan was soon ready as the tent which they had just used and left was being folded and stored on a pack horse. Olga placed herself at the beginning of the group followed by her three companions, first Miramsita with Takuan and then, all by himself, the one from Altan Tobchi, the prisoner who had made his way there from Irkutsk. Raising her arm pointing forward, the Soviet woman commanded the departure and slowly, following the light rising from the east, they proceeded across the mountain, leaving the road which brought them here, cutting across the rolling hills clad in tall, dry grass. The caravan had begun to move again while the grey clouds pushed eastward, the trek proceeding onward, braving the moisture laden winds from the west as they followed the needle of the compass pointing behind them to the opposite, 180 degree position. Ling and Tsur made it known that they had passed a quicksand trap to the immediate east of their chosen route, avoiding it with great concern. Gradually the persistent rain was beginning to drench the leather gear of the animals as well as the loaded sacks and boxes alike. By now most of the riders had covered themselves with adequate repellant clothing; yet, the wind made certain that the discomfort could be felt as the temperature dropped below the pleasant levels, reaching closer than ever before to the zero range of the Celsius scale. It was only five degrees. The

129

sun would once more warm the earth later on in the day reaching the ten degree mark or so. However, the warm days were gone and the ride towards Moeroen would lead them to much higher ground.

The trip began to confront the season and it was definitely time to make the crossover, reaching the main road south of the river bend. In order to travel that distance they had to press onward with only a few rests making four days of riding across this landscape quite a task. Only then would they pause and organize themselves in order to reach the road. Still, from there it would be another full day of travelling before they would contact the main road west of Moeroen.

The long ride went smoothly with only a few not so pleasant surprises. Since most of the horses were not shoed a silent group of riders moved into the day, due south, forging ahead toward the unknown. While leaving their camp on the third morning, the persistent rain, which had been with them since their departure from the Hatgal hills, subsided and a blue sky began to peal itself out of the fog and misery, the endlessly drifting virga disappearing ahead of them, revealing the horizon and with it some enormous mountain ranges.

"Those mountains to our left, over there," began the Mongolian girl, "they are the marker for the river going east!" At that instant the other three riders halted to verify her discovery. A brownish, actually more blueish range presented itself to the onlookers. While the caravan stalled in order to observe the beauty the panoramic view offered to them, a veil of mist raised itself into the turquoise halo where the reflecting glimmer of the early morning sun rays interacted with the rock formation of the range as it touched the light.

"It should only take us one more day to reach the bend," confirmed the White Priest riding up to the side of the Soviet girl.

Nodding, she raised her field glasses. "Well, the range looks closer because the cold air has little movement and offers a very clear image of it. Here, see for yourself!" At this time she gave the binoculars to the *"Russian"* as they referred to the White Priest. Pressing the instrument against his eyebrows the man scanned the horizon and noticed a mass of rising fog to the very left side of the range. After reporting his finding to the girl, she asked for the glasses to confirm what he had seen. "We can now begin to move slightly to the southwest. As long as we have the river in sight from here we can reaffirm our position and take another compass reading!" Reaching into her shouldered leather bag, lifting a wide overlapping flap from above the storage pouch, she pulled the applicable topographical map away from the other stored ones. At this time the Russian moved his horse closer to that of the Soviet woman, thus being able to take part in the studying of the detailed map.

"We have to consider the magnetic variation marked toward the west of us and correct our true bearing!" reminded the girl while pointing on the partially opened map. A few water droplets had previously made their way onto the surface of the map, leaving some distortions on it, which, fortunately, were not made where they had to take their readings. "We should alter our route six more degrees towards the west," said the Soviet girl, mentioning the fact that they had to leave the range well to the east in order to intercept the road near Moeroen.

131

The rolling hills were evenly spread before them, the grass reaching high up against the pasterns of the horses and as soon as the column began to move again, the grass stripped the water droplets against anything that would touch it. The parsimonious looking group began to follow the lead rider whose role had now been assigned to the Russian. Forging thus into the light bathed day alike a group of reborn riders, they made it across the grassland, due south, staying right and clear of the reaching range before them. The Manchurian, the Japanese man Takuan, had placed himself at the far rear, the very end of the trek, where he, minded the troop - and - the company of his friend. They were riding side by side sharing much of their happiness and friendliness with the nearest of the group, shouting across whenever one of them made an observation, moving onward as best as they were able, hoping not to lose much time, thus benefitting from the cooperative weather which had been given to them. The hours were driven by the desire to meet the river bend by the early evening and so, with much intensity, rose and fell the long line of riders as it strung itself over the falling and rising hills south of Hatgal. Soon the sun had risen to the high point under the vault of heaven finding the trek, as it was, squeezing through a defile and upon the entering of it, above the stony breaches of the hill, a throng of tall bluish flowers had spread their forgotten beauty, displaying the fimbriating edges of their blossoms to all those who cared to see them. Takuan dismounted his horse for but a few moments as he went to break a few of them, reaching an array upwards to where the pretty Mongolian girl awaited them. The gesture was well received and well observed by the riders who stopped their horses to look backward when they saw Takuan dismount. The members of the caravan were trained to observe any such unscheduled stop; even if the rest continued on, the group would guard over the stragglers with great care. As the head of the trek moved out of the gorge began the end to enter it. The grassy hills which were flanking it were suddenly lifting themselves steeply into the sky, obscuring the eastern as well as the western panorama of their immediate surrounding. The White Priest, who was still the lead rider, was aiming toward a hill which had a substantial difference in height compared to the end of the caravan.

He halted his horse and waited for but a short while until he could see the animals of Takuan and Miramsita as they emerged from the shadowy path, the bright sunlight touching upon them as if to once more unite them with the rest. Having done so, the Tiger turned his horse away and rode against the steep grade, finally reaching the crest. Being the first up here, immediately, without any delay, trotted the horse of the Soviet girl to his side and thus both the Caucasian as well as the Soviet girl saw the silver line of the distant river at the point where it began to swing from its straight southerly path in a huge curve towards the east.

"Thank heaven!" said the girl. "We have done it! We are right on track, both timewise and in our direction! How do you like that Comrade?" Raising her voice triumphantly, she seemed to expect an answer from the man who had led the way for the remainder of the last segment of their journey.

"I was afraid we were too far to the east but I guess we are right on target!" exclaimed the happy rider.

Since the sun had long since passed the highest point in the

133

firmament, darkness would arrive within the next few hours. The air had already lost its warmth and a few high cirrus clouds began to place themselves between the earth and the sun. Olga pointed toward the sky, "Do you see that? That means it will be much colder tonight!"

"We could stop earlier, say within the next hour or so," proposed the White Priest as he continued to look to the west where a clear, deep blue sky had evaded the high level clouds which placed themselves like a veil lengthwise, running exactly from north to south: between them, the river in the east and the rolling hills on the western horizon. Both riders awaited the arrival of a few more members of the group before departing their concerns; an easy agreement was exacted from them. Olga decided to fall back while the Russian began to point his horse one more time in a southerly direction, pushing his heels gently into the sides of his animal to wake it up. Thus, the column fell into place behind him alike a queue, a winding string of black pearls lying in the high grassland of Mongolia, consisting of a group of human beings sharing together the harsh adventure of horseback travel.

As soon as the entire group began to resume their slow rhythmic pace, the landscape beneath them would also move on and on, monotonously but steadily, consuming time and distance in their given proportions. Before them lay now a wide range, a huge basin, making the animals descend again over a rather long stretch. On a far hill toward their left appeared a huge herd of sheep, thousands of them, being ushered by several horsemen uphill which caused them intense strife, since the herd was spreading itself all over the ridge. As it was late in the year they were probably being herded toward home where they would be fenced in and kept under care until the weather became more suitable for them. Soon the entire column of riders was emersed within the huge basin as it wound itself around an elevation which was obstructing from the west. The knoll was only about a hundred meters or so higher, throwing a pale shadow onto the lower lying ground. Observing this, the Soviet girl pointed suddenly to its crest rearing her horse as she began to ride uphill.

"Look, over there!" said Miramsita addressing Takuan, as she pointed to the horse which was aiming for the top of the flat hill.

"Well, I guess that means it's time to make camp! The sun is getting low," answered her friend, smiling at the happy thought of ending the day's journey, finally leaving the agony of the saddle to stretch, make something to eat and- most of all - to rest.

At this time, as the horse of the Soviet girl began to climb onto the mound, Miramsita and Takuan turned their horses likewise into the same direction. "Let us cut across right now, Takuan!" challenged the Mongolian her closely riding friend. "No reason to waste distance and time. See! They are all turning their animals," ended the girl, observing as to how the entire column had turned west in military fashion, now facing the hill in a straight line. No one, however, spurred their horse for speed after they had been four hours in the saddle so the entire cadre arrived on top with ease and in good time, forming eventually a semi-circle around the leader of the expedition. Olga was thus almost surrounded, waiting for the rest so her announcement could well be heard by all.

"I think this is as good a spot as any," confirmed Olga

135

continuing, "best to stay on the wind sheltered side of the hill here, not on the plateau!" ended Olga, pointing over to the east side of the knoll near where they had come to a halt.

Many voices suddenly could be heard as the lot dismounted and with it mingled the neighing of their horses as they came close to their kind again blending the constant trampling of their hoofs into the melee of sounds. A few animals began to dig with their front legs into the grassy covered hill as if to look for food, giving rise rather to a feeling of their impatience, waiting to be turned loose to find their own food. With the unloading of the luggage much action began to occur: like people seeking out like company. It was not before long that the four friends again came close to each other, beginning to chat, relating to their ride and the observations they made while travelling.

"Did you spot the huge herd of sheep?" began the Mongolian girl addressing the White Priest.

"A hell of a lot of them I thought!" replied the young person asking where they could possibly be taking them out here in the wilderness.

"The government maintains corrals out here to winter them," mixed Olga into the discussion, now making contact as well with Takuan and Miramsita.

"Would you like to stay here together with us?" invited the Manchurian his friends, pointing to a site near them sheltered by a huge rock which was well imbedded into the hillside. Glancing in the direction he was pointing Olga as well as the young Tiger agreed.

Miramsita and Takuan began to unload their animals,

carrying their belongings close to their selected resting place. Having observed them, Olga and the White Priest did likewise. The four persons had finally, without much promotion, found their likenesses and preferred to remain with each other without separating themselves from the group. The now dimly shining sun hurled itself near the western horizon as the time between day and night began to shorten more rapidly with each and every passing minute. Felt sheets were being hung between portable posts, limiting the cutting edge the wind would soon have packing the colder dense air as it began already to drift around the hill. The clanging of pots and pans combined with countless activities all of which are needed to prepare a bivouac. The hustle and bustle was self supporting insofar as one could observe the exertion of the participating individuals: either pulling to unlock the saddle belt or carrying larger boxes about, arranging the ground in order to place the blankets as well as the cooking utensils. Cigarettes were being lit while the first frames for the pots were assembled, the fires quickly to follow, brewing whatever fillings the pots would hold. Soon most of the riders huddled near their makeshift resting places. Since not all were equipped with cook ware, they began to walk over to those who had them, sharing into the entire affair all that which is needed to cook outside. The Soviet geologist Olga, the leader of the expedition, was surrounded by her friend Miramsita and the man who had escaped together with Takuan from the Vostoshnyy Sayan Mountains and, of course Takuan himself. By now hundreds of kilometers south of the Sayan range, Takuan was finally beginning to feel more secure. Being familiar with many of the spoken dialects, he conversed readily in Khalkha, some Korean

137

(Manchu Tungus) and some Oirat and of course his mother tongue, being of Japanese origin. Parts of the Manchu dialect could also be understood by some northern Chinese. The primary European languages remained of little consequence out here, be it then that a sort of poor Russian was spoken; after all, they, the Soviets, had governed the region for a quarter century.

Takuan carried a leather container from his horse to the site where the three friends were engaged in the essential work necessary to make hot tea, thus preparing some needed warmth for their *"shivering insides"*. He began to remove the top of the leather box and was peering into it.

"What're you hiding in that hat box?" questioned the brother from Altan Tobchi of the man who seemed to enjoy having something special.

With a bright grin and a following chuckle, showing deep appreciation for the unknown contents, Takuan announced that he had soaked a special brand of beans. They were not in a liquid but rather lay in a mixture of grass which was moist enough to effect the dry beans but not wet enough to leak through the container. It was a method which was being used in Manchuria. The beans could be transported in a dried state and needed only moisture in order to sprout. By using the dry grass of the highlands and putting it in a leather box, placing it in layers, the beans would soften over the course of a few days. Having explained this to the nearby friends it was the Soviet girl who at once was overcome by curiosity.

"Let me see that stuff!" said the woman while Takuan proudly reached it to where she was seated. Having taken a good long look, the Soviet girl raised her eyebrows while pointing inside

138

the box as if to touch the contents. The Manchurian abruptly withdrew his *"grub"* as if this most precious of foods was about to be contaminated.

"Ho, ho!" came his laughing voice across to her, "These things are delicious if you know how to make them!" ended Takuan, revealing the possibility that his beans could offer a most delightful meal. "You see," began the Manchurian once more, "they've enlarged themselves to twice their original size," said Takuan. "Watch!" In an instant he removed a large brown bean from the box which had its skin broken. He was able to peel a part of the side off it, showing how soft it in fact had become. "They need only a brief cooking time, some pepper and some dried beef and we'll have enough food for all of us!"said the happy rider, as he encouraged his friends to trust him.

The ensuing conversation mixed itself with the comments of the friends to such a degree that much laughter and enjoyment came from it. Happiness in the midst of desolation was a rare prescription for any human soul trying to endure the lonely highlands of northern Mongolia. The evening continued with a contentment which was fuelled by the desire to make the best of the situation at hand. As the daylight was forfeited to the setting of the sun, cold air was rushing in from the south and the summer winds had begun to give way to a new air flow. It would only take another month and the entire plateau would be covered in ice and snow, topping the bitterly cold Siberian winds with those which stream over the plateau, its elevation adding to these winds which can cut, acid-like, into the best covered skin. With the last receding glimpse of a pale red daylight it became apparent that the black icy vault of starry firmament had won the battle. Night had come quickly with the swiftness of the wind which made the horses huddle together in a big circle, heads to the centre, tied to provide protection against the ranging wolf packs. The huge herds of sheep which were kept in the grasslands attracted wolves in large numbers despite the fact that they were being hunted down by horse, car and even single engine aircraft. The group of four had long since tasted the Manchurian baked bean dish, which had been served in only a little liquid glazed with some sugar and a tinge of rather hot pepper. They, all four, were resting near one another and still talking.

It was at this time that the mobile radio made itself known with a rhythmical, high pitched tone, unpleasant and disconcerting in nature. Everyone noticed the piercing sound as the calm of the beginning night was so harshly interrupted. Most of the troop who had already been sleeping for sometime did not adjust quickly to this unexpected and unwanted intrusion. Olga had slipped out of her arctic sleeping bag and hurried at once over to the site where the radio was stored. The rider nearest to it, finally realizing the source of the commotion, removed the protective cover and began to move the toggle switch in order to allow the approaching leader of the troop to listen to the call.

"This is Comrade Olga Likhavchev receiving on special band, independent station G4 near Moeroen," answered the woman.

At that point, while still listening to the receiver, she waved to Miramsita, mimicking with her left hand the sign of writing, indicating that she was in need of a marker. Miramsita had several soft marking pencils in the service pouch which she, alike Olga, shouldered, carrying it always on her body. She removed one of

140

them reaching it quickly to her friend who was listening with great intensity. Exchanging messages was reliant upon the pressing and releasing of the toggle switch, which was attached to the crude metal microphone, clicking it on and off as required. For the moment little talking ensued as everyone waited in quiet anticipation as to the reason for the message Olga was receiving. The less being spoken the easier could Miramsita overhear the conversation. The call was being relayed by the Mondy Station from the Gora Munku Sardyk: a massive station which was built especially high up near its peak, some 3500 meters northwest of the Mondy Valley. That much she could tell from the call sign Olga tried several times to verify. It was, however, extremely difficult to overhear the tinny, flat voice which came over the receiver, since the background noise had still not been brought under control. Miramsita obeyed Olga's gestures as she tried working the squelch knob which finally found a position, thanks to Miramsita, which provided a fairly clear sound over the speaker. Since they had two portable radios with them and since the larger one appeared to have taken damage already, did this, more modern type answer the searching signal from the Mondy-Sardyk station. Takuan as well as his friend observed Miramsita's signals, denoting that things were not right. At this moment, she left Olga and raced a few steps away from the receiver, close enough to tell, hastily, that Hatgal command wanted one of the radios which were assigned to the expedition. Olga, being aware of her orders, had her trip well documented with impeccable papers from the Ministry of Soviet Science endowed with financing propusks, preprinted amounts, folded in a booklet, numbered and perforated, totalling the sum of

141

several million rubles. Most of the Mongolian offices in the Oblast were unable to fill them in the first place; but Hatgal, the old Ugur (now called Red Hero) and also Bulgan (Bulagan) and far south Dalandzadgad were capable of helping out. The reason for this was the fact that these townships were the only ones which sported an active KGB office, and since all matters relating to funds as well as the acknowledgement of vouchers had to be approved by them alone, any traveller could be quickly taken out of circulation. So Moscow had a long arm indeed! After a few minutes the back and forth of switching and talking came to an abrupt end.

"They want us to report, all of us, to the nearest KGB office in either Bulagan or Ulaan Baator," said Olga in disgust, her voice hesitating. She went on to say that a motorcade was awaiting them as soon as they reached the road west of Moeroen.

"To do what?" asked the astonished White Priest.

"I guess they are going to escort us to Bulagan," replied Olga, "or even further. They are in need of our supplies, I was told," continued the Soviet girl. "So, as for now, nothing has changed as far as our plans to reach the road south," sighed Olga.

In the meantime, most of the resting riders joined them in order to hear the news. Many questions were being raised and answered. "What are we going to do with our animals if we are to be driven?" questioned one rider, a Mongolian who had signed on just a few days ago. He continued to say that he was in need of his horse and not willing to become involved in the changes the expedition was undoubtedly to undergo. Discontent spread and, instead of calm, excitement began to set in. More of the men came together to try and make sense of the radio message. Olga knew that

142

she had to leave this question and answer session as quickly as possible in order to have time to confer with her friends. Slowly removing herself from the rest of the entourage, the four came close and began to talk as quietly as possible arranging a felt blanket to guard over weather and sounds, placing it between themselves and the rest of the troop more for the latter purpose than for worrying about the wind. Once this was achieved the four friends drew quickly together as the White Priest began to speak.

"What is it all about, Olga?"

"Well..." paused the Soviet girl for but a second in order to sort out the many things she had been told within the past four minutes, "we are not going to be looking for oil but for minerals, uranium, if you can believe that!"

"Where in heavens will we be able to find that out here?" replied Miramsita continuing to say that in all likelihood they would have to return.

"No, not return, not right now," said Olga. "We have orders to report to Urga first! They will intercept us on the main road near Moeroen. We are to proceed past Bulagan and may not even have to continue any further," ended Olga.

"I overheard somehow that Bulagan has the nearest KGB representation?" began Takuan who had listened into the radio conversation as best as he could.

"We are being picked up, that is Miramsita and I, by truck and escorted to Bulagan or Ulaan Baator," came the answer from the Soviet girl. At this point Miramsita and Olga, as well as Takuan and Miramsita, knew that the next few days would bring drastic changes into their lives. The Tiger, as Takuan referred to his friend

143

from Altan Tobchi, was listening only he had no comment for he realized as well that new alliances had to be made and that they had to be made with great care and planning and most of all in good time - meaning soon.

As the message began to sink in, they could hear the approaching steps of someone. A rider had made his way over in order to be briefed on this latest development so he could give word to the rest of the waiting group. Everyone was on edge especially those who had been hired by the Soviet girl, paid already for sometime in advance, relying upon the willingness of these Mongols to look after the supplies, instruments, tools and equipment necessary to carry out their scientific studies. The Chinese government had, in part, wanted assistance from the Soviet Government in order to harness the finds of oil which were being reported from the far away Shache near the Yarkant River. The disorderly situation in the far western regions could be blamed on the harshness of the civil war which raged through eastern China and since the armies had just begun to change over to civil authorities, little help could be expected from the very young administration there.

At this point, it was being decided by the four to slip back into their sleeping bags, huddle closely together and, being comfortably protected from the cold winds, discuss strategy if there was one to be had. Olga went quickly over with the rider to join the others, to reassure them. She had a happy and pleasant, rather positive sounding voice which, for the moment, was able to put their worries to rest. As it was, the morning was not far away and all were tired and in need of sleep but the latest events had the four

144

friends awake and excited as they began to sort out the newly created problems. Having maneuvered themselves close to each other, it was Takuan who first began to address Olga.

"It looks as if there has been a major change in the attitude of the Moskow office. Oil differs from uranium don't you think?" queried the Manchurian quietly. Miramsita looked at him as their eyes touched for but a few seconds, each of them knowing that their encounter seemed to be coming to an abrupt end.

"I cannot understand the sudden change either," replied the Soviet girl. "We do not know anything about uranium and, as a matter of fact, have no instructions as yet where to look, what new equipment we should require and when all this should take place!"

At this point the Tiger interjected. "Was not the nuclear weapon attack on Japan, August 9th in 1945, the same day the Soviet armies poured into Manchuria?" questioned the young man, as he continued to say, "Was it not after this that the entire political system of the Soviet Union showed signs of nervosity, ambition and drive, hoping to soon duplicate the event, exploding such a device? Am I not correct in assuming this?" ended the White Priest his hasty comment.

"Yes, I can see this as an issue, possibly a reason for intercepting our trip," agreed the Soviet girl.

"Sure, then the rest of the world would again see the great revolution as it had functioned before, more fear, more followers and more conflict!" added Miramsita caustically.

As soon as she finished this sentence, Olga looked around agitated as if to check for listeners. Keeping her voice under good control without becoming too loud, she interrupted, "For heaven sake, watch it! You better get used to the world out here. We are going to be subject to KGB manipulation, new directives and whatever else is in store, things we hardly have time to discuss." Pausing for but a few seconds, she went on further to say that all sounded believable but, just the same, oil and uranium do not mix. "They must have had a reason not to tell us our real mission," concluded Olga almost as if she was thinking out loud.

The four human beings had grown fond of each other during their last days, riding across the wide open land, overcoming many burdens and challenges together. Olga and Miramsita knew the machinations the KGB was capable of and planned with combined effort this trip, removing themselves from the Moskow bureaucracy as they vied, each branch on their own, for attention from those who were able to offer favours to those who could prove their total loyalty over all the others, also trying to garner the favour of the men who turn the wheels. Since they all had been issued legitimate orders, the White Priest as well as the Manchurian had, for the time being, no real concern of being discovered by the *"Green Ones"*. After all, there was no security risk until new orders would be drawn up. For the remainder of the night nothing could be changed or altered anyway. They were in need of rest and had no other choice but to accept that only time would let things develop. Soon all were asleep alike the rest of the group. However, the Manchurian, who had placed himself near Miramsita, did not fall asleep for a long time. They had been engaged in quiet talk, but even though Miramsita had fallen asleep herself now, the Manchurian still was unable to find much rest. He overheard the sound of hushed voices of others in the troop who must have also shared his apprehension as they too tried to adapt to the new situation.

The early morning light began to separate the grass from the scraggly bushes as the shadows gave way. The morning dew had frozen, giving the entire landscape a sugar coating, dividing the taller ones from the shorter ones, the taller reaching leaves beginning to bend from the weight touching the tips of the shorter blades of grass. The horses had fed themselves disturbing the growth wherever they ate, stripping the ice right off the grassland. They were now resting, lying in groups strewn across the hillside. Several riders were getting up. It was time to lead the horses toward the creek which was only a few hundred meters away. As soon as the activity began others joined in and followed, leading their animals along with the rest, saving the water supply they carried with them. They should reach the river bend by mid morning and connect to the main road within the next two days. The terrain was even, rolling away towards the south, leaving high grey brown mountains to their left, the east side. A few fires were being started as life began to return to the caravan. The four friends rose finally and prepared themselves as well as their horses for the final ride, trying to connect to the main road, the one at which they would be intercepted by government agents. Both girls and both men huddled over their early breakfast and exchanged more thoughts.

"From now on let us ride together," began the Soviet woman explaining that it would be better in the event that something unexpected might occur. The rest of her comrades agreed willingly as they, all four, placed themselves at the beginning of the column, leading a lonesome procession through an even more lonesome

147

landscape.

Long before the sunlight was able to infuse some warmth into the brisk morning air had the trek removed itself from their overnight resting place, leaving no clue to anyone as to their whereabouts. The four horsemen led the group on towards the south as the horses were beginning to trot, hoping to make good time in order to find new food and better shelter. Miramsita began to raise her left arm high into the air, telling the following group that a change of direction was about to be observed as she pointed ahead to the southwest. Since the day had well advanced, it was Olga who remarked that it would be sensible to pause, allowing the horses to graze on the pasture, its grasses being warmed by the sun now dripping with moisture, having turned the frost into some sort of benefit. The familiar signs were being given as the rest of the troop fell in, each and everyone being glad to pause, sliding from their saddles, their feet eager to seek out the solid ground once again. The day was being condensed: the longer stretches being seated in the saddle would give way to the very few pauses where men and beast alike were allowed to replenish their energy: the horses grazing nearby; the riders quickly making a fire to highlight the occasion, warmth, rest and food providing all that they were in most need of. The horses had no problem fending for themselves would it not be for the shortage of water. Since the snow had already covered the grassland atop the rolling hills, a dusting at best, was it now too difficult to lead the animals there even a hundred meters. Instead, one of the riders had come back with a leather skin which he had filled with that snow, emptying its contents into a primitive bucket which he then placed over a fire to

148

melt. Most of the riders carried sufficient water along but would not give it to their animals as yet, hoping that they would wander about and feed on the snow which the Mongolian breeds would generally do on their own. The interlude did not last very long and the group of four did not make much ado about it. Their conversation with the others in the entourage was kept to a minimum being busy with themselves, seeking distance from the rest in order to use the moment to relate to each other. The radio message had become a problem for them since it renewed the uncertainty the Muscovites were so familiar with. Miramsita as well as Olga had already had unpleasant encounters with the Ministerium of Internal Affairs during their university days. This part of the government is strictly controlled by the KGB or in fact is the KGB itself: that type of Political Secret Service which had a reputation for harsh measures and spread a silent fear, like a huge blanket, over the entire population. During their ride the four had agreed that they would take a *"wait and see"* attitude towards the meeting with the officials, when and if they indeed should be intercepted by them on the main highway towards Bulagan.

"The radio message was rather confusing," began the Soviet girl addressing the closest of her comrades, Takuan, who had pulled his horse alongside hers. "They seemed to have little concern about the rest of our group. I cannot just let them go: everybody has made arrangements to stay away for a year or longer. Their entire employment was secured with the permits of finance for that period of time!" continued the dark haired Soviet girl as her voice became considerably louder. At this point Miramsita's gesticulations caught the eye of her friend. They did not wish to spread anxiety or distrust. Everyone was listening in order to catch anything, trying to overhear any part of the spoken word which was able to offer a hint as to the plans the leaders of this caravan had in store for its members. Ling, the Chinese rider, had come closest: he addressed the Tiger with unusual cordiality mentioning that it was a hard ride but that he was doing better than he had done on the previous days and was looking forward to reaching the road and learning of the meaning of the new *adventure* awaiting them.

When the White Priest related the comments to his friends, it was Miramsita who said in utter disgust, "We do not need any adventure coming from the government people. The less we have to do with them out here, the better!"

Having heard this Olga agreed, "I cannot help but distrust these administrators. They always are a step ahead of you and they plan around you, you know," thus verifying her fears, recalling previous experiences which quickly came back into memory. They indeed lived in the Stalin era and though much has been said of the man very little would be spoken about him whenever more than two people were present. The Secret Police had infiltrated every phase of *Soviet life* and trust was something which was impossible to come by. "I am certain that they intentionally gave us a cover, creating the oil exploration story, back home," concluded Olga. "This trip was established with a disinformation order. It is not oil they are looking for, it never was in the first place!"

It was at this moment that Miramsita drew very close to Olga. She placed the tripod cooking frame on the ground as she replied, "Yes, I wondered as well but dismissed the thought because

150

all our gear, all the information we have been carrying along with us, pertains to the finding of oil. But I think you have a point, Olga!"

Takuan was also listening to the conversation of the two girls. He had distinct concerns pertaining to his background. His friend, the young Tiger, as well as he had become a part of the entourage, hiding their true background, happy when they succeeded in leaving their past behind them by attaching themselves to this group. Here, they suddenly received documentation, papers which were of the utmost importance if they wished to succeed in their escape from their past, knowing all too well of the long arm the Secret Police had across the vastness of the Union of the Soviet Republics. It was true that the distance from Moskow produced a more relaxed attitude in the brethren, but both knew that this was purely a matter of self deceit, *"highly psychological"* as the one who was referred to as the Tiger so often described it. The Mongolian towns out here were not very large, in two respects: the population was not of any significance nor was the area which the townships held large in size. Ulaan Baator sported a few high rises which were being financed by Moskow. More workers had been employed here for sometime now and the building of housing was continuing on a slow but steady pace. The landmark of the old, stern yet serene looking Shaman Temple offered a strange contrast to the white high rise buildings which began to mark the skyline with their scaffolding. Raw looking, clinical, they opposed the temple and the entrenched concepts out here. The new had come; yet, nobody could tell what this modern look would hold in store in terms of the future. The passage behind the temple was lined with

151

prayer wheels, many of them, smaller ones as well as rather large ones. The newlyweds would still come here and spin them after the ceremony in their temple was over; but, yes, a new element was growing within Ulaan Baator. One which was related to concrete, a rather crude, cheaply designed complex, housing large numbers of people. As more workers were being brought here more drinking occurred and the Yellow Hatted lamas were beginning to dislike the new influence. The old name Urga had accepted the revolution rather well, renaming Urga to pay homage to the spirit of the *Red Hero*, thus calling it so. Bulagan, a town east of Baator, had a KGB office since it had a larger postal station. All remote post offices were being manned by KGB officers. It was fairly easy to control a community that way. The mail always supplies an ample amount of information to anyone who cares to take an interest in it. The envelopes are being stamped with date, name of city and sender. The post offices were equipped with *silent letter opening devices*, either using steam, chemical solutions or soft lifting techniques to gain entrance into its interior without revealing to the citizen that the information therein had been read. Unwelcome, anti-government opinion would result, eventually, in deportation. The *Gulag*, that is the north eastern part of Siberia, could accommodate thirty to forty million prisoners. They either worked on government projects or were simply held to whither away; especially if they were deemed to be politically untrustworthy.

All this was well known to the four friends whom faith had found and begun to bind together with each ensuing day, slowly but surely as the hoofs of the horses made their way south bringing distance between them and the *new workers' paradise*. Having such an emotional background to share, it was only a matter of time until they all sensed this common bond within themselves, especially when unclear radio signals came across the air waves. Anything not so clear was definitely understood as being very suspicious. Bulgan, the closest of the towns having a larger post office, was referred to by the Mongols as Bulagan and the Mongolian riders seemed all to pronounce it, as it sounded. Being instructed to report to that town in itself would raise suspicion in all *"those who knew"*.

As the pause was coming to an end the four riders had found enough time to chat with each other and also relate a feeling of happiness and carefreeness to the rest. This, so decided the four, was essential in order to retain the services of the group for the time being. The light snowfall had signalled the beginning of a change in weather and since one day out here can become a dividing power so gigantic in possibilities, no one who knew this land would hesitate very much. Thus, the trek resumed its activity. While the four lead riders made their way past the waiting group, the rest, slowly and safely, fell into the line as they saw fit. A few of them were still dismounted, extinguishing the fires which were made on the ground, stomping on the embers until they gave no further signs of activity. The great huddle, the clump of horses and riders as they were still together, began to uncoil into a long black strand, engraving the grassland with that sight as the caravan moved into the final day, the day before they should encounter the main road.

Miramsita and Olga led. They were riding side by side, talking with each other as soon as the terrain would allow them to remain close enough to make an exchange of words possible. "We should reach the road sometime tomorrow in the early afternoon," speculated Olga. "That is if the weather holds," she added.

At this time Miramsita nodded her head, confirming the concern Olga had as she looked also to the southwest. "The wind has become rather icy," said Miramsita quietly, as if speaking to herself.

"Here, I have another lambskin I do not need right now," said Olga, feeling that her friend was not dressed warmly enough for the remainder of the trip. Miramsita agreed and not much time passed before Olga was able to undo a saddlebag from which she freed a good sized parka. For but a few moments both horses halted as Miramsita slipped into the jacket, then, resuming at once, they made their horses trot for a few dozen meters in order to make up for any possible loss of time.

The convoy stretched itself outward about a quarter kilometer behind the four lead riders, alike a black string of pearls strung across the landscape. A few of the riders wore snow jackets, thus interrupting the black string of pearls, putting here and there little gaps in it. Miramsita began to speak of her relatives in Choybalsan, located near the Kerulen River which flows close to the Manchurian border. She had an uncle living there. Choybalsan lies west of the Manchurian border, Manchuria offering a rather interesting landscape on its west flank. A fair sized lake lies between the Mongolian town and the Manchurian town of Hailar, interspersed with swampland on the higher level, Hailar offering an airport between Hailar and Nantun. The Soviets secured it when they entered Manchuria forging from Choybalsan across the border,

154

taking it in the first week of the hostilities.

The next five hours were passing rapidly, the riders having now difficulty staying close to the leaders who were determined to make distance before all would halt one final time for the evening rest, readying themselves for a cold night to come. By now the group had been directed much more to the southwest, staying clear of the high plateau, hoping that the next day would find them in a steady descent to the main road near Moeroen. During the entire ride on this day they did not spot one herd or any herdsmen. Most of the sheep were by now in winter quarters, still in the open air but under protection from the inclement weather for which most local travellers had a fearful respect. As the evening began to approach, the dull, grey sky was alike a dome of mist under which a dozen or so courageous riders forged onward as if to prolong the day by sheer effort alone: an effort which aimed toward clarification of a status quo - a condition which rested heavily upon the chest of the four lead riders more than the grim, unfriendly weather did. The southern range was being obscured by the inclement weather conditions but, all considered, the misty ceiling did not depart any of the snow it quite easily was able to hold. The landscape offered little encouragement: it had not changed noticeably and provided none of the pleasures a tourist would wish to remember. No one here used his camera in order to record the sights which were nothing but an object of hindrance to all involved. The rolling hills still had not produced one single tree within the last day of their ride. It was this monotonous picture that had implanted itself into the souls of the group who appeared as if they were on a mission to map the unknown, a country that once had enclosed a group of

155

people who would race across the earth, leading their wild horses westward, entering Europe, filling the books of history with the smoke and carnage of a conquering horde of warrior nomads. As they had arrived from nowhere, in the minds of the Europeans, was this nowhere to be found right where the tired troop was about now moving, driving their horses southward towards Moeroen.

The young one whom his friend referred to as the Tiger, was riding beside the Soviet girl, when he, following a gesture from the Soviet girl, turned his horse around so that it would face all the riders who were eagerly following them, all of them waiting for the sign that camp was to be made - finally. As the lead riders waited, the rest of the convoy arrived, everyone happy for the pause and everyone tired enough to ask no further questions as the routine proceeded to unfold, beginning with the dismounting of their horses. The familiar sound of horses neighing mixed with the sighing of the human beings so perfectly that it had become the noise of contentment to the ears of the travellers rather than anything else. The clapping and banging began as well, as each and every person readied themselves for the meal, thinking of the darkness which was soon to fall in. They were late and the ensuing night would not wait at all but began to unfold its cloth of darkness, highlighting the flickering fires against its background. Everything which was happening had a routine measure to it and it was not before long that the last noise subsided as the mealtime faded into the resting time. The transition from the one to the other occurred so smoothly that quiet set in more rapidly than ever before. Since the weather cooperated, all was going well as the tired crowd consumed the well earned sleep in a rather effortless manner. Even

156

the four friends would quickly succumb, resting deeply without that any further talk was able to take place. During the last portion of their ride they reminded themselves that they should, just to remain prepared, rehearse the entire discussion they had, one more time. In doing this, they thought that they could discover any error or oversight, thus remaining well ahead of the situation. However, being deprived of their much needed rest and because of the demanding ride they had subjected themselves to, exhaustion became the victor. All four were soon soundly asleep.

The night passed thus rather quickly as the new day began to announce itself in the east: blue sky bespeaking of hope. The horses, resting as they were, remained calm as not to disturb the arriving morning which sent a bright yellow band of light ahead of the sun, still trying to climb from behind the horizon. Some of the hills in the distance showed a touch of icing upon their grass covered tops, while a larger one was covered with a dusting of new snow.

Takuan, who had placed himself near the Mongolian girl, was the first one to introduce unrest as he began to free himself from several layers of blankets, headgear, scarves and other things he was able to use to keep the heat in his body. Since everyone else was still asleep, he continued to rise with more caution, hoping not to disturb his friends, all of whom were resting as if the night had not ended as yet. The Manchurian enjoyed the early hours of the day as he always had since he was young. Walking about, he approached his packhorse, stroking its forehead and petting its shoulders. He was content doing it. Then slowly he began to walk away from the animal, climbing, steady in pace, the shallow hillside

157

which they had used as a protection from the cold, southwesterly winds. The grass proved to be slippery as it was covered by hoarfrost. Since the cover was rather unevenly distributed, Takuan was able to reach the crest of the hill without too much trouble. From here the clear weather allowed him an expansive view, his eyes probing past misty regions which were of an isolated nature. The land showed its vastness as it sloped downward toward the southwest, touching upon sky and ground at the very same time. He noticed the many hills as they differed, some of them clad in the white of snow which must have fallen recently, others yet totally untouched by it, while the hills to the east of his position were covered in brown grass, showing little or no sign of the white frost which appeared to be everywhere else. Miramsita must have sensed the absence of the Manchurian. She rose from her resting place and looked about, seeing him as he stood there. Both soon interacted, each having caught the eyes of the other. Both waved and thus acknowledged each other's presence. Right afterward Takuan was about to leave his position in order to join the camp when his eyes detected several black spots which appeared to move across the white landscape. They were to his far right and were moving in such a manner as if they were constantly passing each other. He counted four such spots and observed them with some interest. After a few moments they, all of them, made a great big semicircle to the west as they disappeared from his view. At that moment he dismissed the picture in his mind and began to walk toward the campsite, happily thinking about the girl, looking forward to chatting the first words of the day with her. She as well began to walk towards him, slowly, interspersing her steps with brief pauses,

158

rather letting the man shorten the remaining distance between them.

Within the past minutes the rest of the members of the convoy had found their way back into the new day. The night was over and the morning activity saw to it that no further rest could be afforded. The horses began to become restless while their handlers were being reminded by them of their duties. The final ride towards the main road was about to take place. Having this in mind all hurried along with their activities as tea and bread, oats and dried fruit were being prepared for breakfast. Wrappings and cartons were burned for the needed fuel and, most of all, to eliminate the crowded saddle space. The scene was almost similar to that of bygone times would it not be for the undertone and strange tension, that of facing uncertainty, something any human being dislikes.

Takuan was still descending from the hill while Miramsita waited for him. As soon as they were close enough to each other one could detect their happiness, each offering to their counterpart a warm smile of welcome.

"Thank heaven," began the Manchurian, "this night wasn't too bad, cold enough all right but bearable."

"Well, you must have been rather warm, you got up early," joked the girl.

"I got up because I was losing warmth! Seeing the first sign of day I decided to check on my horse. Then," while pointing over his shoulder, "that one hill gave me enough exercise to make me warm." At the very moment the Manchurian spoke his last word a loud, roaring noise made both turn their attention to the south. "That sounds like a plane!" Takuan, now scanning the sky, was trying to locate the sound.

"It is too low for an aircraft," answered the girl. By now all of the members of the team followed their instincts, looking up into the blue morning sky in an attempt to identify the source of the noise.

"It's a biplane!" came a voice shouting across the camp. "I saw it pulling up past that hill over there!" One of the riders pointed to the southeast side of their campsite. The roar became undulating whenever the pilot pulled the nose of his machine up before he dropped it right after, making the motor work hard only to relieve it from the strain by tipping the aircraft forward. Then, very suddenly and abruptly, an aircraft shot over the crest of the closest hill, spooking the horses in such a way that they reared on the spot where they rested, kicking and flailing their limbs about in a frenzy.

The joyous excitement turned into an abrupt panic. The silhouette of the biplane disappeared as quickly as it had presented itself, still buzzing around, diving and maneuvering about in a carefree manner. By now, everybody was running toward the horses, some of which had gained their much desired freedom with their first try, pulling on the loosely tied reins, disengaging them, galloping across the grassland away from the hellish intruder. Most riders were quick to overcome the stunning performance of the carefree flyer, unless they were willing to walk for the rest of the journey. Takuan and Miramsita, who were the first to gain control over their horses, proceeded to aid the rest to recapture their celestial mounts. Then the aircraft returned once more, flying dangerously low, prompting one of the horsemen to discharge his rifle. The powder puff was climbing straight into the air, marking the place from where it had been discharged.

"It's a damn R5 reconnaissance!" yelled somebody into the air from the place where a group of the furious were still congregating, running about without their horses. Any coherent conversation had long since ceased while the aircraft made another, low pass, this time flying about three meters above the ground, following a depression, being in fact beneath the campsite, exposing its structure from the top - a lonesome pilot driving the machine in an ardent fashion amidst the turmoil as if he was trying to round up a herd having first succeeded in driving it into a frantic panic! Upon an attempt to raise the nose of the biplane for a steep climbing maneuver, its motor began to sputter, leaving a blueish black mixture of smoke beneath its wings, only to recover its perfect running rhythm a few seconds later. The incident must have reminded the pilot of the limitations of his machine as he banked sharply, aiming south from whence he had come in the first place until no further sound could be heard.

Takuan, Miramsita and the White Priest were riding in a huge circle, heading off a few of the horses which had successfully gained a respectable distance from their campsite. With the disappearance of the plane it was not too difficult to regain control over the situation. The animals were soon rounded up and herded back. In the onsetting panic the horses had trampled on the gear which was now strewn all over the place, the damage apparent whenever their hoofs had stepped upon a box or blankets, soaking them with freezing mud and grime which resulted from the abuse, soiling almost every item that rested on the ground. With most of the riders by now having returned, harsh words and even harsher curses, for which the Russian as well as the Mongolian languages were very well equipped, spanned the distance between the excited ones. The four friends had finally come together and, alike the rest, began to discuss the incident.

"If this moron needs flying lessons he should practice somewhere else!" scoffed Miramsita.

"By the way he was flying, it appears to me that he can fly rather well," cautioned the Tiger, adding that this person could easily be a scout for the party which was to intercept their convoy near Moeroen. Having voiced thus his opinion, the rest began to quickly cool their anger. It made sense and everybody knew it.

Takuan, who had exclaimed that he would skin that pilot, changed his attitude noticeably. "Well, he certainly can't think very much of us!" observed the Manchurian. "Passing so low over the campsite, knowing we're on horseback."

"Lucky we were not!" said the Soviet girl. "Some of us would have taken a bad fall." The Manchurian and Miramsita agreed.

"It sure was instant chaos," verified the young Russian.

"I told you, Miramsita," began the Manchurian again," I saw four dark spots from the hill, remember?"

"Oh, yes, I remember," acknowledged the girl, "but, you only mentioned it briefly as if it was not important. Let us ride back up and have a second look!" At that moment the Mongolian girl turned her horse on the spot, galloping away, racing to the top of the hill, quickly being followed by the Manchurian as well as the young Russian, whom they all began to call Tiger. This was because the Manchurian referred to his friend often using the name

Tiger, remembering bygone days. Soon the rest of the friends, knowing little about the origin of this name, simply adopted it since it appeared somehow to fit the personality of the young Russian. The Mongolian woman, excited as she was, reached the hill far ahead of the other two, while Olga instead turned away in order to attend to the rest of the group. It was, however, only a matter of seconds before both men arrived near her. Miramsita was still trying to control her horse. It had more momentum than it needed and took some handling in order to convince it to succumb to the wishes of the rider. A threefold silhouette marked the spot on the crest of the hill, the horses halting but dancing around their rear quarters obeying the harsh message from the reins. The head of the Manchurian's horse lurched wildly up and down, its mane opposing the motions as it rose and fell with the changing of the pace, causing the rider to force the animal into obedience by using the reins in a rather strict fashion. In but a few short moments all animals adjusted to the pause the riders sought. "See! Over there," began the Mongolian girl as she pointed into the sky towards the south, "that is the same plane which was just here." Both men acknowledged the sighting and found the four dark spots on the terrain exactly as the Manchurian had said.

"It appears that plane has a purpose," cautioned the Tiger. "Watch! It's circling overhead back there."

The Manchurian digested the image, shading his eyes with his left hand, thus concentrating. "Yes," began the friend, "two of the dots aren't moving any longer. I can see only two right now. Where are the other two?"

"Oh, you needn't worry. I'm sure they're somewhere close,

probably hiding in a depression so we can't see them!" scowled the Tiger. "But I'm certain that they're communicating amongst themselves," continued the Tiger. "That aircraft is still flying close to them. It's just coming up for another pass, see!" The young man pointed in the direction where the aircraft circled, ever so often disappearing whenever one of the distant hills came between them and the flying machine. At that moment, they all saw the aircraft while it was flying quite low aiming higher into the sky and then, banking rather harshly as if to stand on its wing tip, it straightened out in a flat line disappearing to the south.

"Well, so much for that!" said Miramsita. "He has left."

"But *only* he has," began the Manchurian his conversation which was intended to remind his friends that the four dark spots had become larger as they aimed north toward their campsite.

"I count now four moving targets," started the Tiger as he went on to say that they were moving in their general direction. "They're about an hour's drive away from here," concluded the young man, verifying with the others that they ought to ready themselves for a visit, break up camp and do all the essential things: meaning that the four friends would keep together; that the brethren, that is the Manchurian and the Tiger, would rehearse their stories; in short, that each and every observation of the past had to be put into perspective. The new documents which the brethren had received from the Soviet girl were held ready for an eventual inspection by KGB officers, who carried with them almost unlimited powers out here.

"Well, I better ride at the end of our group," began the Manchurian, looking at Miramsita. The Mongolian girl, having

164

sensed that his background was rather questionable, coming from Manchuria, speaking better Japanese than Manchurian, knew that they had to talk in private. The young Russian, sensing this, removed himself from the scene advising them that they should stay together, close enough for any unforeseen event. This was essential if they were to remain aware of the situation at all times. It was to be expected that, as soon as they made contact with the government agents, their caravan was in danger of being dispersed. This could happen in many ways. The leaders, the Soviet girl and the Mongolian girl, could be sent somewhere else once their old instructions were replaced with new ones. The others could be ordered to remain in the district until their identities were verified by the KGB. This was the established rule, the functioning chemistry of the Secret Police. The citizens of the great state knew of this and accepted such behavior as being normal: meaning that fear had become a part of everyday life. It was, therefore, that most citizens learned not to talk very much about political affairs, especially if more than two people were present. The disinformation department of the KGB would entrap its citizens. It was known that political prisoners were deemed to be the worst type of criminal within that system and subsequently received the harshest punishment. Many people were betrayed by ambitious agents, those who hoped to *"get up in the ranks"*; thus selling out their best friends for political gain. No employment in the great state was more secure and better served than government positions. Miramsita and Olga both belonged to government established unions. All professions were organised into unions but these establishments, themselves, did not adhere to any democratic order.

A union leader was appointed until the party saw fit to remove him. On occasion women were leaders of such union groups; but they as well had first to prove party loyalty. In short, the system functioned as it was known. This meant that if elections were held, it would pay to vote in accordance with party policy. The KGB had mastered the art of eliminating anyone who had the courage to oppose, dissent or even propose better or different ideas for any given argument. Being well equipped with such knowledge, was it then that Miramsita and Takuan began to suddenly speak openly and very quickly about their future. In the meantime, the trek was being led onward: the Tiger and Olga had placed themselves at the front, guiding the long queue of riders south.

As soon as Takuan and Miramsita found a gap within the column of riders they began to talk. Having slowed their horses to a canter, a speed which the Mongolian horses seemed to prefer, they showed an easy, rather relaxed gait. Miramsita now opened the conversation.

"We have been together for but a short while and, I think, grown fond of each other's company. The radio message to Olga seemed to indicate the end of our togetherness," began the girl, pausing here for a few seconds, sighing briefly. Takuan, who had been staring straight ahead, now turned and looked at the girl and, as their eyes met, they both new at once that they had been in love from the first moment of their first encounter.

"I know," was all the Manchurian was able to say as his hand reached across touching her arm, while both horses went on about their task faithfully bringing their riders toward any destination they had marked for them.

166

"The caravan is watching over us," smiled the girl as she endured the touch of the person who had become so dear to her. Meanwhile the sound of an approaching horse reminded them to disengage. Miramsita quickly withdrew her hand, while Takuan switched over to touch her saddle flap, pointing to its lining which appeared to show the opening of some stitches, just in time to give the newcomer a thought other than the two lovers had with the comfort of their touch.

"How come you are riding all by yourselves today?" began the one who had suddenly appeared from behind. The Manchurian was swift in his answer but casual enough to parry the inquisitive approach, saying that their horses were related to each other and preferred riding side by side than following. It was one of the more likeable Mongolians who had been hired by the Soviet girl and who had, so far, seemed to be enjoying the trip. He was telling them that he was about to join up with Olga and that he was looking forward to reaching the road by the evening and as he departed as swiftly as he had arrived, he shot away on his *celestial mare* digging both heels into the flanks of his animal, shouting a sort of *"hurray"* to himself, his horse flinging bits of earth into the air as if the frozen ground was made for better traction.

"That is silly!" began Miramsita. "The hard ground going uphill can injure its fetlocks." Without looking back, the rider moved quickly to the next group in front and once again slowed his horse, making himself known, apparently talking while passing them as he had done previously. Riding along slowly as they were, they found themselves to be the last ones.

"Oh heavens! He was the last rider. I guess we are about to fall behind. I never noticed," exclaimed the girl.

"Yes, I know," said the Manchurian as he pointed ahead. "Look, two of them aiming back here."

"They are not. They are going to our right as if they intend to cross the hill, see, there," interjected the girl. At this point in time both riders were about to reach the flat top of a wide, grassy hill, losing, at the same time, sight of the two horsemen who had just vanished over its skyline. Being shielded and totally alone, separated from all, their horses touched as both lovers halted their animals. The Manchurian embraced his girl while they were still in the cover of the nearest hill, hidden from the rest of the entourage. They would stay there for but a few minutes. At that point in time they both agreed that they would remain together, thus organizing their affairs in the event that the Secret Police would learn of the true origin of the Manchurian who in fact was an offspring of a mixed marriage. His father was a Japanese officer, having settled in Manchuria after retiring from the army, marrying one of the local beauties near Harbin. It was because of this background that they had to avoid any in-depth questioning by the KGB staff, should there be an interrogation. This depended entirely upon the mood and circumstances as they would unfold. The KGB remained unpredictable in their actions since most of the procedural mechanics depended entirely upon the character of the person in charge.

With the coming of the evening they should arrive near the main road. It was now that they had to square away any existing problems. The Mongolian girl was well aware that the Manchurian did not speak any dialect fluently. His partial knowledge of their language as well as being able to speak several Chinese dialects, yet speaking none of these fluently, gave rise to the suspicion that his mother tongue was somewhere else to be found. Trust, a most rare commodity in an unfree society, would quickly bridge the gap between lovers. Takuan made his past quickly known to his girl who told him that much of what he revealed to her had already been silently suspected by Miramsita. Both riders would soon leave the protection of the hill, speedily cutting the distance between them and the rest of the troop. Tiger, as well as Olga, noticed their absence since the tip of the convoy climbed over a rather steep saddle, allowing them to oversee the entire troop as it lay between them and the end.

Chapter VIII
The Siberian High

The signs of the beginning of an early winter were well observed by the leaders of the caravan. With the falling of the first, light snowflakes, a subconscious type of hurrying had set in. Moskow had given their complete backing to the expedition: meaning ample financing to allow for the logistics including arranging for a change in the event a different mode of travel should be required. Three thousand kilometers of riding, as it was planned initially, appeared to be slow and unproductive. Olga as well as her friend Miramsita knew that they would have to change over to another, faster mode of transportation. This was to occur as soon as they had crossed the first high plateau. The Great War being won, the reparation payments were now being spent on new ventures alike this expedition. Therefore, many funds were available to encourage oil exploration. Miramsita and Olga were aware that the region of Surgut, which was much closer to Moskow, had already shown promising results. In fact, it was learned that more oil was expected to be found here than anywhere else in the entire Soviet Union. In spite of the massive reparation payments, which saw the dismantling of thousands of well functioning factories, the Soviet Union was money starved: it had no foreign currency for the essential international trade and the recently won war offered little reprieve for the cash starved nation. Olga as well as Miramsita had spoken

170

often about their mission. As they reviewed their previous experiences, as they laughingly referred to their mission, the entire venture retained the same elements of mystery throughout. From the very beginning to the present it truly bore the touch of an adventure. Receiving the last radio message, however, caused them to think and to change their carefree ways becoming much more cautious in the assessment of their mission.   After all, Joseph Stalin was still firmly at the helm: meaning that any plan or any change thereof could be revoked at any moment in time. Nothing remained truly stable in terms of planning.   Uncertainty still reigned amidst a nation which had extended its borders to such a degree that the far flung machinery of the administration had to be overhauled rapidly in order to avoid a collapse in the economic structure as it presently functioned.   The radio message also taught both girls that although they were far away from Moskow they were still accurately monitored in spite of the distance which had, at no moment in time, separated them from this mechanism of surveillance.   During the war years harsh penalties for non compliance with any government order found the disobedient citizens quickly banished to the *Gulag*, the dreaded labor camps which buried more human beings than Soviet soldiers had died during the Great Fatherland War and that number was in excess of twenty million fighting men! However, the victorious ending of the war did not bring about a relaxation of government pressure upon the population at large. The masters of the state were set to duplicate the scientific advantages the Western World was able to provide. The explosion of a nuclear device, as was used against Japan, catapulted a frantic effort throughout the Soviet state in order to bridge that gap. Olga as well as Miramsita

171

knew that their mission was being halted and they had the distinct feeling that, from the very onset of their travels, the truth was not to be found in the search for oil but rather in the plan to secure uranium deposits. This venture, of course, had to be shielded from the prying eyes of the international community. Disinformation, an effective and well established methodology of the Secret Police, would account for their oil exploration marching towards the far West, remaining all along close to the borders of the state. It was by now obvious to the four friends that changes were in the making. The uncertainty as to the nature of these changes spurned an uneasy feeling in all of them.

During the last segment of the route the four friends were able to converse sufficiently. They had planned and discussed certain main issues, such as how to account for the extra hired help. The documents of each and every one of the parties who had been assigned at a later time to the very same convoy were verified and double checked for error. It was now up to the government which appeared to have sent the aircraft in order to spot their whereabouts and intercept the expedition before it made the big turn west. The last discussion between the friends dealt with the radio message and whether it had been sent in a confrontational manner. The conclusion to that discussion was of a more positive nature. It appeared the caller did not know very much about the logistics of their expedition and seemed to be simply echoing an order across the wire. The fact that the aircraft appeared in the fashion in which it did, flying low, making many large circles over their camp, to view it, made them feel, to say the least, extremely uncomfortable. It was obvious that the pilot must have spotted the animals as well

172

as it was evident that he did not care very much about the discomfort he caused. From such behaviour alone was it possible to assess the frame of mind the government officials must have had when they sent the aircraft. Olga was of the opinion that it could have been the plane of a higher official, perhaps a military officer refreshing his skills using an old R5 reconnaissance biplane: one which was no longer included in the military inventory. Having reviewed all these possibilities, they decided to wait and see: a method which was, during those days, well adhered to in the Soviet Union.   As soon as the lead riders reached the last high promontory, they were able to see far ahead. Beneath lay a huge, flat area, white, resting under a thin layer of snow which had just fallen a few hours earlier. As the Mongolian girl reached the point first, she drew her horse sideways so her friends were able to position themselves to her right. All of them were awestruck. Before them, not more than two miles from where they halted, sat the aircraft surrounded by many trucks, small ones and larger ones, crowded with many people who dotted the landscape like the sheep did just a few days earlier.

"Just as I told you," sighed Miramsita,"they are waiting for us all right."

Olga looked through her military glasses and began to count, "One, two, three.." Then being silent for a few seconds, she announced that fourteen trucks and five jeeps were parked near the aircraft.

At this time the Tiger reminded his friends not to show any anger regarding the flyover, the one which had literally scared their horses to death, thus giving the Secret Police a starting point from

173

which to use their influence. "Remember," cautioned the White Priest, "you're far from home and there aren't any Moskow courts out here. You'll just conveniently disappear on the next census. No one will know where your last contact was or who spoke to you." Having said this, the rest of the riders filed in, clogging the landscape in such a way that the other party downhill could not help but take notice.

"Well, good luck then," and with these last words OIga commanded her horse to go on, leading her caravan down from the last elevation directly toward the assembled crowd, the ones who had it in their power to direct all of them to new destinations. The last of the riders leaving the mound experienced a remarkable sight, their trek winding toward the low lying land, gradually losing height, descending to the grassy plains of the region. It was as if the past began to mingle into a new era. While this transpired two smaller Jeep type vehicles proceeded to separate themselves from the immediate vicinity of the parked aircraft.

"Oh boy!" began the one whom they referred to as the Tiger, "Here they come!" Takuan had spotted the vehicles at the same time. Olga and her Mongolian girlfriend also indicated by gestures that they too had noticed the approaching Jeeps. Two of these American built vehicles, out of an estimated 41,000 which were given to the Soviet Union during the Great Fatherland War, somehow had made their way into the remote regions of "*Outer Mongolia*". It should be only a matter of minutes until these vehicles would arrive to confront the lead riders.

Olga waved to her friends in an assertive fashion to come

174

one more time close, calling loudly across to them, "I shall ride ahead! Let me intercept the first Jeep. Do not exchange any words with them and confuse them as to who is leading this expedition. Make sure and let me do the talking!"

The White Priest relayed the message to Takuan, who was near the young man from Altan Tobchi. Takuan quickly made the words known to Miramsita. They were now ready for the encounter. The first of the two Jeeps had in the meantime raced with great elan toward the riders, closely followed by the second vehicle. The leading one was white in colour, its black tires contrasting its structure in which only two persons appeared. Both of them were clad in the familiar Soviet Army snowshirts, their dark leather gear offsetting the persons in a sort of official frame-work. As the two vehicles careened toward them, the wildly turning tires were grinding the earth and snow into a brown dirt, spitting it high up into the air behind them, twirling the mess carelessly about as if to tell all of their rank, power and importance, assuring an arrival which could not easily be overlooked. At this moment, the first Jeep had come close enough to pull sideways slowing its speed considerably by a skillful shifting maneuver until it came to a full stop approximately ten meters from Olga's horse. Having noticed all this in great anticipation, Olga had brought her horse under good control observing the driver, who, as soon as the vehicle had come to a standstsill, flung himself out of his seat, missing the steering wheel and clearing the chassis of the Jeep all in one sporty movement. A tall, slender built white Russian, after collecting himself briefly, began to walk slowly but firmly, in measured steps, toward the first horse. Olga could clearly see that

175

his facial impression was an energetic one, stemming from a person who was accustomed to being in control. As the man drew closer, it became apparent that he was of mid age. He carried a side arm on his left side which was pushed forward to rest between the belt buckle and his left hip. He wore the standard army type fur cap, the side flaps loosely dangling over both of his ears, the late afternoon wind tossing them about as it pleased. Olga decided to extend the greetings first, thus forcing the officer to accept a prevailing, positive mood, apparently coming from the leader of the caravan.

"Good afternoon, Comrade!" smiled Olga, trying to squeeze some extra words into her introduction.

However, the Soviet officer interjected, thundering back, "Welcome Comrade to our region. I am Colonel Joseph Nakhimov with the Ministry of Internal Affairs. I am here to escort you to Ulaan Baator." Having so said, he began to close the gap which was still between them. As soon as he was near enough he reached up to aid the woman who was by then trying to dismount in order to repay the greeting. Helping her, he got his first close-up look at the woman who offered a bright, inviting smile, sufficient to disperse any existing animosity. After hesitating for but a few moments, the Colonel reminded himself of the old patriotic habit, carefully embracing the girl, kissing her by gesture only, first on her left cheek, then on the other. Simultaneously, the girl replied in kind. The contact was made in such a way that all fear was being put aside, at least for the moment. Olga proceeded to introduce Miramsita, Takuan and the Tiger, telling jokingly that he was a white Russian of the Cossack tribe from Rostov na Don. In fact, neither Olga nor Miramsita knew of his true background, which was overshadowed by his friend who referred to him as the White Priest: the person he met not being a priest per se but rather one who possessed the skill of a superior fighter. In concert with true Buddhist tradition only a priest, in the mind of Takuan, would be able to have such an in-depth knowledge as his *"Tiger"*. Henceforth, the name Tiger was established with admiration firstly and then, as time went on, the name became a casual reference, simply serving to identify someone who was different, novel in many ways. The Colonel seemed to only have heard the word *"Cossack"* and was very pleased, at once yelling the words Taras Bulba, speaking with much enthusiasm about the great liberator of his people, thus addressing the *Tiger*.

The White *"Russian"* used the inviting enthusiasm of the officer as a bridge toward understanding, moving his horse close enough to reach for the extended hand of the official saying, "I, Colonel, rather believe in Taras Shevchenko, the poet who opposed Peter the First. In any event, Gogol tried to show that great courage is always needed to guide a people!"

With this statement as an opening, the officer smiled and began to praise the great courage of Marshal Stalin, making everyone cringe, though secretly of course. A few of the nearest riders were verifying the great glorious achievements of their Marshal and fell into praise, setting an overall happy tone, making the encounter one which would direct peace rather than hostility into their previous worries. The rider who made the comment began to produce himself noticeably, pressing his horse past the bodies of others who had come to join in the introduction. He was of

Mongolian lineage and introduced himself to the Colonel as Iskuel Tamu. Olga as well as the rest of the crowd, which had by now congregated, took notice of the rider since he never spoke a word, remained well to himself and was generally known to be quiet, minding his business, being engaged with his own activities. It was noted by the four friends that he was suddenly capable of conversing rather well. Not before long was it then that the man climbed from his horse, walked over to the official government agent and began to introduce himself further.

"I am proud to meet someone at last who represents Moskow out here," affirmed the rider, engaging the officer unexpectedly in conversation, thus interrupting the events which had just unfolded. The tall Colonel turned totally away from Olga and her party, one more time telling his name and rank, offering these courtesies as a casual greeting procedure, now evoking the response of the *"nervy"* horseman, who continued saying, "My name, Comrade, is Iskuel Tamu, former officer of the detachment in Irkutsk, accompanying the group as you may have heard!" The following few seconds of silence which prevailed were enough that each and everyone near made the right assertion in an instant. The rider was from the same Ministry: he was in fact an agent of the KGB assigned to the group without revealing his true identity to them! It was the first surprise of the trip: a revelation about the state of affairs by which the country was governed, controlled and maintained.

"Did you hear that?" whispered the Tiger to his friend Takuan whose horse had come close enough to allow him to hear.

"Can you believe that!" mumbled the Manchurian, equally

speaking under his breath, looking straight ahead, addressing his friend in such manner as to not reveal to anyone who would observe him, that he had just spoken. While both agents were still conversing with each other Miramsita observed how the quiet rider Tamu had changed his attitude toward his companions as he directed one of the horses nearest him to turn away. The animal had brought itself innocently between the two men and the waiting Jeep, much to the annoyance of the Mongol. Still talking, he grabbed the leather leading to the martingal, forcing the head of the poor animal backward with such strength that it shied, rearing around its left with such a sudden jolt that it almost threw its rider. Olga was about to interfere when Miramsita, who happened to be lengthwise of Olga's animal, reached swiftly across, poking the horse, forcing Olga to first pay attention to her mount who was by now very agitated. In so doing, Olga was able to observe the facial gestures of her friend, instantly reminding her to remain neutral. The facial sign language stemmed from previous such experiences both girls had encountered in the past and worked if it was done while no one was able to observe it.

"Whatever doom or fortune leads, one age the hero, one the poet breeds." Having thus spoken, the newly established Cossack smiled back at Miramsita, whose courage and presence of mind had just saved the day. Olga had dismounted and was holding the reins of her horse tightly until the unruly animal was brought under control. At this point the tall, interesting looking Colonel, told his comrade in arms to rest, raising his left hand sternly toward him as if to push him backward. This movement occurred with sufficient speed to invoke an abrupt silence.

179

"Your name Comrade, again," began the man, addressing Olga directly, as if he had forgotten it in the ensuing turmoil.

"Olga, Olga Likhavchev Comrade Colonel. I am responsible for the logistics of the caravan," answered the girl.

"And who is in charge of the scientific part of your expedition?' came his question back to Olga.

"I am and Doctor Miramsita, Colonel," replied the woman while correcting herself in saying, "The native comrade, as a matter of fact, is our Comrade Miramsita, Colonel!" The latter words revealed all that which the Mongolian girl was able to keep from the rest. Takuan as well as his friend the Tiger, whom the Colonel had just called the *"Cossack"*, took immediate note of that particular part of the introduction of Miramsita.

"Well," began the KGB officer, "we cannot stay here all day! Comrade Miramsita, you come with us. Give your horse to one of the riders to hold. The rest of you..." he pointed toward where the other riders waited, "go on to our camp. You can see it from here!" Having said this, the Mongolian girl was ordered to accompany the Colonel.

The word *"doctor"* caused the separation from the four friends and it was now important for the remaining ones to keep alert, trying to rectify the situation as time went on. Olga exchanged but a few more words unable to recover, knowing that she had committed an error. One never volunteers any information too readily to the Secret Police, especially not to a high ranking Secret Police officer. As the Mongolian girl began to climb into the vehicle, she turned to her left, casually waving to her friends who were still struck with silence and inactivity in the face of the sudden development. The Colonel placed himself behind the wheel and it appeared as if he enjoyed driving, throwing the clutch into action in the same high spirited manner he had when he arrived. In only a few seconds it was wheeling around and away from the caravan, aiming straight to the "makeshift camp" he was talking about during his introduction to Olga.

"Well, let us go there, right now," began Olga while mounting her horse. She was barely in the saddle when her horse already began to lead. She waved to her friends to come to her side and both of them immediately understood. It was not clever to talk too much or even to talk at all. The Mongolian rider was still with them. He was obviously displeased with the Colonel who seemed to show little interest in what he had to say. Having revealed his cover, the rest of the troop began to avoid him. This in turn would make the undercover agent feel more out of place since the Colonel, his kind, left without paying due attention to him. The three friends had placed themselves in front in order to quickly bring distance between them and the closest followers. This being achieved, it was Takuan who first was able to exchange some words with Olga. Soon the *"Cossack"* had closed the gap as well, being now able to partake in the brief conversation. Takuan and Olga had quickly agreed that everything depended on a swift follow-up. It was vital that they shorten the time the Colonel was able to spend alone with Miramsita. The slower they travelled the more time the officer had to secure his information or give orders which would remain uncontested by Olga, the person who had been given the exclusive rights and powers for this expedition.

181

"Don't go too fast, Olga!" cautioned the one they would from now on call the Cossack, speaking as loud as he was able to. "We don't want to show concern, otherwise they'll suspect we have a reason to worry!"

Listening, Olga slowed the canter of her horse down to a trot. "Do you think so?" questioned the girl.

"I know so," answered the Tiger, while Takuan added his version, arguing that not too much time should be spent, since the drive by car would give a definite advantage of nearly ten minutes to the KGB man.

"He'll already begin barking out orders while he's driving!" shouted the Manchurian angrily to his friends. It was at this precise moment that they heard a horse approaching from behind them. Takuan at once thought of the other man, the agent, the Mongol; and, looking swiftly back, identified him as the one who was approaching. "The creep's coming!" warned the Manchurian his friends who had already recognised the oncomer without actually looking at him. Pulling to the side of the lead riders, Iskuel had problems with his horse. He had come to the front so swiftly that his horse overshot, showing poor horsemanship on his part.

Making the best of the situation, he called across to Olga, "What is your hurry, Comrade?" Waving her right arm downward, she commanded all to slow the speed of the ride, thus eliminating the noise of the many hoofs which, hitting the partly frozen ground, made a splashing sound whenever soft snow came under them.

"We are not in a hurry my friend but, as you can see, my horse is!" replied the girl.

"Of course, Comrade, they know it's feeding time once

more!" In so saying, the Mongol adjusted to the mood of the Soviet girl.

"It appeared that you were passing us, not we passing you!" mentioned Olga in return. Takuan and the Cossack observed the man as he tried to begin a conversation.

"They're putting up tents, see, over there!" interjected the Cossack.

"Yes, they are better ones than we have. Those tents are good for fifty below. They are from the department!" boasted the Mongol proudly, indicating to his comrades that he was in fact one of them, one of the few and that he was indeed well connected.

Takuan, his eyes contacting those of his friend, knew they shared the same thought. This was the kind of character who was known to be dangerous: the type that is often found in the political arena, advancing through keen observation, feeding on ambition, adaptable and sly, being thus bred by a combination of many things, acquiring a skill for survival not found anywhere else by trusting peoples.

The Mongol uttered a few very excitable words which no one was able to grasp as he moved away, hurrying to arrive before the rest, suddenly leaving the group behind, hoping to ingratiate himself with his superior. The group of friends had by now been warned through his actions. They would watch him and not give him any reason to cause them harm. The short distance to the campsite was soon bridged by their constant speed: the horses sensing the pause which was inevitably connected to food.

As the day had advanced already into the evening hours and since a special kind of uncertainty waited for the group, the diminishing sunlight added an extra dismal mood to the scene. It was Takuan who approached the first tent which had been erected amongst many others that were still in the process of being raised. He halted near it until the rest of his friends filed in to either side of his horse, bringing their animals under control in order to dismount them. The three friends decided during the last few moments of their ride that they should approach the first tent, hoping that the first structure to be erected would belong to the Colonel. Before they dismounted, being high on horseback as yet, they could observe a gathering of many trucks, American GMC types. The *"Cossack"* was able to identify these three letters. One of the trucks was facing in his direction, the letters emblazoned on its grill. The trucks were enormous in size, sporting a twofold arrangement entailing a front portion, the cab, having on its back a huge mounting on which a long loading surface was being hooked.

"Well," began the Manchurian as he observed his friends' reactions, "they've definitely thought of everything!"

"Yes, indeed, it looks like we won't have to ride out of here!" came his friend's swift retort.

The events began to unfold more rapidly than they had begun. The good looking Colonel came from inside the tent as he opened the loosely hanging flap, flinging it to one side, hence presenting himself in his full stature, tall as he was, wide shouldered, clad in his covering snowshirt across which the dark leather work proportioned the rest of the figure, dividing the top from the bottom by the horizontally worn belt. His long legs were well placed into huge, white, felt boots. A shoulder strap, which

184

found its way from the very front to the rear of the dark brown leather belt, in general, identified the wearer to be an officer. Out from under his fur cap darted two dark brown eyes, friendly in nature, should the situation warrant it. At least for the time being they were still inviting, as his gestures parallelled his mood, one of his arms reaching out, beckoning them to come in. By moving aside the loosely hanging canvas which covered the door opening, the three riders, Olga, Takuan and the Cossack entered the dimly lit space of the tent. Miramsita, who had been waiting with great anticipation, had risen from a large bench, a foldable type: one which would collapse if one knew how to bring the mechanism into motion. The girls were happy to see each other so soon and it was this moment that Takuan used to casually step close enough in order to relate to her. As soon as everyone had entered the tent, a soldier busied himself closing the entrance, tying the loosely hanging flap to the rest of the canvas enclosure. The soldier, also clad in a combative winter uniform, snow shirt and all, was unarmed. He appeared to be the aid to the high ranking officer. As he lit the gas powered lamp all the attention of the group was taken by the light source which began to gradually become brighter until, with the ever increasing pressure of the gas, a white, glaring flame centered in the top of the lamp. The intense pressure of the escaping gas produced an eery hissing sound indicating that its function had been achieved. The inside of the space revealed two square tables, a group of light chairs, the large bench being mainly occupied by a round tent stove to which a type of army canteen was attached, leaning against the centre support pole which parallelled the stove pipe leading to an inset fire guard through which the pipe escaped.

185

The oven was well heated and produced a noticeable warming effect without that its steel sides revealed the source of the heat. It was not glowing as most of them do, since they can be easily overheated. A momentarily induced disorder prevailed until the Colonel himself found an opportune moment, asking the four friends to be seated. He invited Miramsita and Olga to one of the tables and directed the two men to the other one, while he, himself, elected to sit with the women, not beside them but on the smaller end, allowing the girls to be close to each other. The gas lamp was placed on the middle of the table's surface and began now to illuminate it, revealing a large map, writing utensils and writing pads. Within a few moments all had been seated awaiting a statement from the person who had intercepted their expedition. As the men removed their caps and gloves, the short cut, dark brown hair of the Colonel revealed a large scar which ran from his right eyebrow about four inches in length into his hairline, giving him the mark of a warrior.

Colonel Nakhimov had readied himself sufficiently to begin. "Having heard from Comrade Miramsita, I believe your mission was to link up near Onjuul, south of here, there to intercept the east west road to the south of the Bayasantgaan Range, re-equip your group and move on in a southwesterly direction, through the Gurvan Sayhan Mountains, using local people to guide you across them, correct?"

"Yes, Colonel, correct so far," replied Miramsita while Olga verified her words by simply nodding in affirmation.

"You are geologists, both of you?" At this moment he directed his attention to both girls, looking at them in order to confirm once more that which must have been revealed to him through government channels in the Department of Internal Affairs in Moskow.

"Yes, Comrade Colonel, we are both geologists," replied the Soviet woman, looking directly at the officer.

"I see. Well, we do need citizens of your knowledge in our fight against the monopol capitalistic forces." Pausing here for the duration of but a few breaths, he resumed, "I was instructed to inform you that your previous plans are to be changed. You will not be travelling on to meet with the Chinese contingent of scientists in Yarkant. Instead, you are to take part in a top secret endeavour which shall be revealed to you in Ulaan baator. The extreme secrecy of this venture will begin with the clarification of your personal background." Pausing again, he looked around in order to find acknowledgement from the other persons inside the tent. Takuan and the Cossack as well, were careful to immediately show an eager interest in his words, causing the officer to relax and resume his deliberations, announcing that they would leave in the early part of the coming day. "We have arranged for trucks large enough to safely accommodate your horses," boasted the officer, waving to the soldier who sat in the half shadow of the brightly shining lamp, producing himself suddenly holding a framed picture of one of the trucks with the Colonel behind the wheel. The man reached the picture across to the officer and upon changing hands, the Colonel turned it towards his guests. "See, this is one and we have five of them with us! Take it!" The officer invited the nearest person to him to reach it around to the rest. Miramsita, being closest to the Colonel, was the one who accepted the framed masterpiece. The picture was an enlargement of one of the vehicles

187

which was taken from a diagonal frontal view, giving the officer the central seat, so to speak, in the picture. The long box at the rear of the truck appeared to be twice as long as it should have been. As the picture made its round, it was carefully handed along, Olga finally getting up in order to reach it to the men who were close by but seated on a different table. The mumblings and gestures of quiet wonder and admiration were executed with such finesse that the Colonel began to enjoy his position much more than ever before. Takuan knew that this was the opportunity for the placement of some well put questions. He quickly proceeded to take advantage of the moment and asked the KGB man whether age would be a barrier in the event that a new recruitment was to take place. Being directed in such a way the Colonel began to address the entire group of assembled persons.

"First of all, I have as yet not indicated that any changes are being planned. The matter, that is of the new assignment, as I mentioned before, will be evaluated once it has been determined as to whether all of the present comrades are deemed trustworthy enough to remain with the group. We have been given a new assignment and, in accordance with the requirements of this assignment, rules must be observed. My duty is to ensure that these rules are being adhered to." Pausing here, he drew a package of cigarettes from beneath his snowshirt, parting it near the top so that he might find the chest pocket in his undergarment. He offered them to his comrades and found no one willing to smoke until his aid appeared, sharing one of them with him. This at once eased the tension which by now was beginning to make itself known since the four friends were eager to assess their situation.

Takuan and Miramsita were still fearing a separation, while Olga as well hoped that their expedition would remain intact. After all, the girls had planned the trip from the beginning in such a way that their togetherness was never put into question.

"It is possible that we can solve our problems in Moeroen," said the Colonel, sensing that the four members of the caravan were showing signs of tension. Their lack of conversation became dangerously obvious since none of them seemed able to readily adjust to the situation in which they were being maneuvered. The Cossack, sensing this, was frantically searching for a better topic that would stimulate a more intimate conversation. It was important to engage the KGB man and crucial for his friends to learn what was being planned for them.

"I believe Moeroen has a weather station Comrade Colonel. Since the present weather could worsen, it would be nice if you could arrange to clarify our situation. We've been in the saddle for many days now and would sure enjoy a rest."

Having given the Colonel a reason to speak further, he rose from his chair, briefly stretching his stiff shoulders by forcing them backward. After he had strutted a few paces away from the stand he took a deep draw from his cigarette and puffed the smoke out through his nostrils, still hesitating with his answer. He suddenly turned back and stopped as he began to speak.

"You are the Cossack, are you not?"

"Well, you could say that I've had experience in that region, Comrade Colonel. I can however not claim that I'm responsible for the heroism which was being shown there a hundred years earlier!"

"Nonsense!" thundered the Colonel back at the White

Russian. "It was still your kind who began the first uprising against the declining rulers, these well mannered puffs who never did much for anyone other than live off the rest of us!" The Cossack previously observed that the Colonel had made notes while addressing them. They were made with his left hand. Such scrutiny led to the answer as to why his pistol was placed on his left side. Military dress code disallowed such a liberty unless a sound reason was given for the circumvention of such regulation. "We have no security clearance as yet for either you or your comrade and, frankly, I am afraid that you must remain with us until all that is done."

This was what they needed to know and, finally, the KGB officer had released more information than he should have. It was now certain that their documentation, that which stemmed from Olga and Miramsita dating only a few weeks back, would undergo a thorough investigation. Since the documents were filed by radio and since they were arrived at while travelling, the primary parts, the pictures of the two friends, were not available. The lack of passport photographs alone would give the two friends freedom from further probing. For the time being both had bought another 24 hours before their clearance would be challenged by the KGB. Neither Miramsita or Olga had asked for the peoples' pass. Each and every different region in their vast country had picture passports which were colour coded. For the most part, only the KGB knew of the coding. The capital of Moskow was identified by a different colour from another city or region. Anyone fleeing or transgressing the coded zones unwittingly was subject to certain arrest. At this point, it appeared the Colonel, by seeing the men

190

together with the two leaders of the caravan, assumed that clearance had been given back east.

"For the time being, I suggest that we all get some rest," continued the officer his conversation. "I forgot that you have been in the saddle for a long time now. My aid will show you to your quarters, both tents are close in the event that you have to share cooked food together. By the way, your horses are being cared for by our people. You better rest well because tomorrow we will have a long journey ahead of us. For the time being you are all under my command. Thank you, comrades!" Having thus spoken, Joseph Nakhimov quickly killed the burning cigarette by pressing it against the metal lining of the round oven, smiled and gave instructions to his aid in order to also provide time for his own rest: that is to say, not only rest but food as well. Within a few moments the four friends left the tent following Corporal Tarassov who took the lead. The Colonel followed them to the exit and spoke a few words, saying that they would see each other some time in the morning and that he would send his aid, maybe even have breakfast together. The Corporal, showing the way, offered to carry Miramsita's shoulder bag which was rather large and appeared to be heavy. She graciously declined his offer preferring to guard over her precious cargo. Both tents were close by and smaller, at one point the canvas sheets touching the sides of each tent. Tarassov drew open the entrance for the two women and asked them to proceed inside. However, both had stopped to observe how a group of soldiers was still active erecting another more distant structure, which was round like an igloo, resembling the shape of a Mongolian yurt. The men decided to enter their tent at once. It was important to them to indicate to the Corporal that they were minding their business, that nothing was going on which would warrant an immediate discussion amongst them, certainly not outside. This could create suspicion since most of the KGB staff were well trained in the observation of all the peoples who came into their sphere of influence.

The snow had stopped falling but had still laid a substantial blanket of crystals over the frozen soil. A group of KGB soldiers was busy caring for the horses. They had in fact driven them into a makeshift corral which consisted of four giant GMC trucks, surrounding them, leaving little space for the animals to escape or, by the same token, to be contacted by their former masters. It was obvious to the astute escapee from Irkutsk that certain precautions were being taken. What was unsure was whether it was a routine arrangement or the result of a specific order. As the men began to secure the entrance to their tent, it was Takuan who caught sight of the Mongol Tamu as he left one of the horses belonging to the caravan, carrying the radio along with him.

"Hell, look!" began the Manchurian, making his friend quickly take notice of the act, both men shutting the entrance flap with immense speed to ensure that the Mongol did not spot them. The tent was sparsely lit, showing two army cots which were equipped with numerous blankets. It would take only a few seconds more before both friends were able to see clearly into the depth of the enclosure. It was Takuan once again who would begin the conversation, while his friend was still engaged in the process of familiarizing himself with the inside. "This is incredible!" but before he could utter another word the Tiger swiftly covered his

192

mouth with his outstretched, flat hand, using his right index finger, bringing it vertically across his very own lips, commanding silence. For but a few moments his friend showed anger wanting to continue shouting about the Mongol creep who had just confiscated their radio. Fortunately, the *"Cossack"* was able to point to a wire which ran straight through the far end of their tent blending well with the shadow the oil lamp threw toward it. The wire was difficult to spot. A blank portion, less than a quarter inch in length, had revealed its position as the flickering light touched it thus exposing it for a fraction of a moment, long enough to send a flashing spark toward the young Cossack discovering the intruder. They quickly made their way to it, following its path. It was leading into the tent of the girls. Both friends were unable to detect the listening device which had to be attached to it. However, a wooden crate, empty of Vodka bottles, had been thrown against the tent's cover hard enough to disturb the line. Takuan began at once to scribble words of warning on a piece of cardboard. He swiftly left the tent, entering the other soundlessly, finding both girls still standing, discussing loudly their dismay. The Manchurian knew that someone was trying to spy on them and repeated therefore the same gesture to the women which he, himself, had just received from his friend placing his right index finger across his lips while reaching the cardboard over to Miramsita who began to decipher his message at once. Takuan was not certain how many observers were busy spying on them. For the moment, they were sure that the Mongol Tamu enjoyed nosing about: quite a change from that person who had been with the caravan always demonstrating a gentle tendency in character. It was interesting that he seemed completely unaffected

193

by the knowledge that his comrades felt deceived by him. Even though the crew deliberately began to avoid him, this fact appeared not to influence the self-consciousness of the man whatsoever. This lack of concern about revealing his identity was a warning to the four friends who had well observed and better adapted to what they experienced. It was for this reason alone that Takuan did not spend any additional time with the girls, knowing they had caught on. They would trace the cable and begin to revise their conversation to cover any previous errors they might have made, misleading the Secret Police in the event that their conversation was being monitored. The Cossack was busy looking for any other indicators which might provide him with more knowledge as to the type of surveillance technique being used against them. While he was busy lifting blankets and moving cartons about, he was pretending to talk to his friend who had actually left to warn the women. He kept on simulating the conversation, saying, "Hey, easy, easy now. You seem to be tired. Are you dizzy? Sit down and rest for a moment! Breath easy, all right? ...and one,..and two, and three, much better." He acted out the presence of Takuan, pretending to breathe as well, inhaling and exhaling noticeably though still careful not to exaggerate. KGB personnel were specialists and not to be underestimated in their professional training. Within the next few seconds the Manchurian returned from his mission, nodding, indicating that the message had been delivered and, most of all, that the girls had understood. As if this was not enough excitement, Takuan was now being faced with more as he observed his friend's stupid behaviour, pointing at his own chest and then to that of his friend who finally understood the

194

charade. The Manchurian began to mimic the gestures of the Tiger and finally came around to the part where he had to speak.

"All right, all right, I'm fine. I'm just tired. I think I turned my head too quickly and just got lightheaded." It was a blessing that the friend had caught on to this performance, just in case *"Big Brother State"* was engaged in any theatrics. It was very dangerous to fall under a type of continuous suspicion. Since it belonged to the good tone to be under observation, the long time, the endless time of observation was, however, one which would result from small errors. Even the slightest reason to extend a government surveillance, new and repeated flaws, gave any underling a chance to prove his loyalty to the system. He would joyfully proceed to embellish the file. A branded file was readily used for verification and follow-up procedures until the entire picture began to blur, changing from fact to fiction. Many Soviet citizens lived out their lives in the Gulag camps of northern Siberia because the result of such fiction had sent them there. *"Russia was great and the Czar far"* was the saying of the previous generations. Now the people could say that the KGB is near because of the dossiers it created and kept.

The two friends immediately continued, now engaging in a casual discussion, speaking of the last day, while feverishly searching for any device which could invite the ears of the KGB. Takuan placed a chair on top of a few stacked boxes, then climbed onto it, looking straight upward, lengthwise along the center tent post to where it passed through a rounded mount. Standing their for a few seconds, he then climbed down just as nimbly as he had gone up. Takuan indicated to his friend that he had found a small microphone beside the outlet for the pole. It was obvious that the first cable had no connection to it or if, that the connection was being made outside, either on top of the canvas, or was woven directly into the covering material. It was not before long that both friends were able to isolate a seam which appeared to have no true purpose. It had to be the one which led to the microphone! Upon further examination, pressing the seam from two sides, it was the young Tiger who indicated to his friend that he was now certain the seam was filled.

"The wire... touch here," invited the Tiger his friend. The seam ran straight from the top alongside a fold near a zipper down to the underside of the tent, remaining just a little above ground level.

"Leave it alone!" whispered the Manchurian, speaking with a low voice.

It was now obvious that it had become almost impossible to converse. Both men agreed to a casual, aimless discussion, complaining about the long trip and the weather, never missing, from time to time, to praise the great ideals of Marxism. It was decided not to undress. The temperature could fall dramatically at any moment, something each and every native Mongol knew and respected. Both friends had learned much from what they were being told and had ample experience with the northern winter near Altan Tobchi. Once the shepherds removed their animals from the plains, they knew winter would soon begin. They had seen many such signs during the last days of their journey. The nearest tent to their own was that in which the girls were. Both men had noticed in the outset, that the bottoms, the bases of both tents opposite from where one entered, were touching. It should be possible to bridge that distance easily by simply pushing a stick under the edge until it entered the other tent. Takuan had a long bamboo stick tied to one of his boxes. Freeing it, he proceeded to do precisely this. The cane-like stick began to push away the thin layer of snow on the surface of the soil and was able to get under the grass, finding soft earth as yet untouched by the penetrating frost. The grinding sound of the device was difficult to hear and Takuan, in an attempt to gain the attention of the girls, kept on moving it back and forth. They were certain that they had to only concern themselves with a distance of less than a meter. Half of the stick had by now penetrated into the other space.

"For heaven sake!" shouted the Manchurian under his breath. "What is it with these women?"

In order to provide a good sound profile for their activity, the ongoing conversation between the two men had to make sense. It was obvious that someone was listening intently into the privacy of their world and it was also certain that this had begun as soon as they all entered their tents. While Takuan still was engaged with the stick, agitating the soil repeatedly, he suddenly paused, standing up, freeing himself from the crouched position in which he had operated having one knee on the ground while trying to manipulate the stick. At the very moment he sought reprieve from the unpleasantly held posture, the stick began to slide away, disappearing into the other tent. They had obviously made contact. It was now of the utmost importance to maintain a casual conversation. Not even the slightest error was forgivable if they

197

wished to remain in control of the situation. Both men knew that the girls were well equipped to outmaneuver the antics of the State Police. The everyday citizens of the *"Peoples' Union"*, the members of the workers' paradise, were little schooled in the methodology of the KGB. The people had a healthy respect for them which derived from the absolute powers they were given. Many lowbrow officers, who rose through the ranks during the early days of the revolution, had by now secured such powers. The revolution had created a massive disorder in the administrative offices. Hardcore criminals, even many murderers, suddenly found their way to freedom, using the unrest the revolution so conveniently offered. As files were lost, burned or willfully destroyed, these people were well equipped to ingratiate themselves with the new leaders. The top ranking elite of the KGB had many such unsavory characters amongst their leadership. In Moskow, for example, rumor had it that the chief administrator Lavrencia Beria, would drive through the city at night collecting pretty girls for himself, throwing them in a holding tank for his deviate activities. One day, he accidentally kidnapped the daughter of a Soviet general, so goes the story, which subsequently began to cause him serious problems. Yet, in spite of these criminal activities, later years saw this person rise to one of the leading positions in that country.

The Manchurian and his friend had many occasions to talk about the motivation of the young intellegencia tracing the history of the system as it unfolded. Living for the main part off theories, political theories, they became the repeaters of something which was largely unproven. The machinery of the Soviet Union as it functioned, economically, morally and ethically, revealed great inconsistencies. The people at large were heavily motivated, their minds almost totally controlled using the latest concepts of modern psychology to praise and propagate a doctrine which was that of dreamers not telling their masses that ideals have to be financed. Chez Gueverra, the Cuban revolutionary, could not inspire the simple villagers, many years later, for his cause. They were more interested in knowing who was on the weekly, rotating passenger bus serving their village than anything else. No one told them that their living standard was being devoured by the immensity of their large offspring, leading to massive pollution, lack of employment and food, not to mention disease and other setbacks. The dogma of the church had more powers of persuasion than the revolution had promises for them. Grave error lay in the high mindedness of the idealists who saw the world as they wished to see it rather than observing how it, in fact, functions. As soon as a state succeeds in destroying the incentive of its population, disallowing ownership, better pay for better work, the most basic and most natural structure of any society, such state and society will become obsolete in its message of betterment. Having a moral background in such observations, all four human beings learned, over time, to retain an independent intellect which was very much hated by the government, so much so that lifetime sentences were handed out against such functioning thought patterns.

As time was ticking away rapidly, so did it also appear to be standing still. With their silly conversation continuing, it became apparent that both men had to speak louder, for any words which were uttered too loudly made it easy for the intercepting listener, by the same token, any words not understood by the very men who spoke them would breach the same line of communication they had to have in order to function themselves. The tent began to move: the front flap, tied as it was, tore at the mounts. A nasty wind had suddenly invited itself into the setting. The Cossack peeked cautiously through a tiny opening near the entrance.

"Wow! Blowing snow, lots of it! Come here," beckoned the man. Takuan dropped the paper pad which he had just unpacked and ran over to his friend eager to look for himself.

"General Winter, my friend... a godsend!" in saying this, he clapped his hands joyfully striking his friend on his shoulder as he continued his cavalcade of words. "We can speak now. They'll be busy, too much noise in here.." hesitating a moment he went on "...and out there!" By now they were able to hear the piercing sound of car horns as some of the vehicles began to reposition themselves trying to shield the main tent, the one in which the Colonel stayed. Takuan was quick in suggesting their own action.

"I'll go over and talk to the girls. You make some noise in here. I'll be back in a jiffy!" Having said this the man was gone, the Tiger helping him untie the tent flap. Takuan needed to speak to the women who had been without contact to them for too long now. It was important to learn from them what they had said the few moments before the listening device was discovered. Takuan made the assumption that the tent of the women was equally rigged, allowing the intelligence crew to construct traps, word traps, laying snares for later ambushes in the event that an interrogation should take place.

Takuan mentioned to his friend that his mother, who was

born in Manchuria, had a sister living somewhere in the southwestern part of Outer Mongolia. This thought entered the mind of the Tiger without that he understood its significance. In the meantime, the Manchurian was busy within the girls' quarters. His uninvited appearance caused only a minor interruption. The Manchurian saw the bamboo stick in Miramsita's hand. She had already wrapped a note around it hoping to push it back with the much needed information. Within the short time in which the parties were separated, so learned Takuan, the Mongol, the very person they feared to be a spy, had returned the portable radio pack. Tamu used the occasion to warn them of the microphone in their tent. It was sitting inside the hollow part of the supporting pole which was the main device holding up the roof. The interesting part of this deceitful plan lay in the observation that the microphone in the mens' tent was comparatively easy to spot, while the one in the girls' quarters was expertly hidden. Tamu was able to hand to Olga the official order for the arrest of both the Tiger and the Manchurian. The order stated in plain language that both men are considered to be escapees: the Manchurian a Japanese officer, the German, a young soldier in the possession of damaging information regarding the Soviet government. Before the Manchurian had finished reading the information, he was already crossing back to his tent to find his friend waiting at the entrance. He held the document so high it almost touched the face of the Tiger who was trying to read the few sentences. In the meantime, the wind began to howl much more violently than before while a strong gust tugged on the main struts holding their tent, bending them under the onslaught.

"Did the girls learn any more about the Mongolian?" questioned the Cossack his friend.

"Yes," answered Takuan. "He belongs to a Chinese family in Kumul which is on the other side of the Altai Range. They were incarcerated when the Holy Buddha in Ulaan baator was put under surveillance." He, Tamu, exclaimed the excited Manchurian, belonged to a clandestine group of only a few souls having succeeded in climbing up in the ranks of the KGB. The most important thing he reiterated to the girls was the fact that they had to get out, using the turmoil to do so. The ever increasing wind was now entering the storm phase. The soldiers were too preoccupied with keeping things in order which meant that they were running about retrieving rolling cartons, watching over the trucks and other vehicles and most of all attending to the tent of the Colonel which had been thoughtlessly placed on much higher ground, and was thus taking the full brunt of each and every gust which came its way.

Both men left together in order to see the girls. As soon as they entered the enclosure of the structure, they began to talk. "First," ordered the Cossack, "cut the lousy wire. Now!" Takuan had his long combat knife hidden under the left side of his parka. It flew out of its mounting, stabbing the seam, puncturing it as he cut efficiently across.

"To hell with you bastards!" was the first thing he yelled into the space, "Now we can talk." This accomplished, other ideas came quickly into being. Miramsita spoke of the radio.

"The weather.." she said, "there is going to be a report on it, I am certain."

"Go ahead, get it by all means!" agreed Olga.

The radio pack was hurriedly freed from its canvas housing, and not before long, seconds only, the first green light steadied itself indicating that it was getting warm enough to become functional. A few squealing sounds found very high and low notes until the squelch was properly set. Miramsita listened into the night.

"I got it, I got it..." For but a few moments everybody was as silent as the rest of the noise permitted. Miramsita had the ability to remain undeterred: she listened long and hard and then began to talk aloud as she received the messages. "Intense low pressure moving in from 290 degrees to 110 degrees, wind velocity to increase to 150 knots by the early morning carrying large amounts of snow...Weather warning extended for 36 hours. Affecting the region from the Voshny Sayan to the northern perimeters of the Gobi Desert...." At this moment the tent flap flew open producing the Mongul Tamu in its very center, hesitating only momentarily before entering. He embraced the Mongolian girl and began.

"I must enter. I cannot be seen outside. You have to move tonight. Everyone is busy now as you can well imagine. Use your maps and equipment, it was meant to last you for at least a month anyway... now get going." While the man spoke, and as it was obvious that time was of the essence, little interference came from anyone. They were all listening. Nothing could be chanced at this point and trust had to exist before all. Any unnecessary argument would literally steal the few precious moments they had.

"Miramsita," began Tamu again, "you come with me later on. You know your animals."

"And what're you going to do later on?" dared the Tiger to ask the Mongolian man.

"Not very much my friend, but enough to get you on the road!" Pausing here, he collected his thoughts. "Can you drive one of the big rigs, those GMC trucks out there?" Tamu suddenly asked the startled young Cossack.

"I think so. I've driven a small bus," came the answer back to the Mongolian.

"Well, you better be able to Cossack! If they catch you, you will be good for forty years way up north. You cannot get far in that weather with your animals, but, on the other hand, your animals can go where they cannot." Pausing here for a few seconds, the man continued, "My plan is to observe the weather. As soon as the visibility gets less than 20 meters, and it will, you have to get your horses on one of the trucks. Use the one parked near the flat dirt road. I was told it is solidly frozen all the way to the south from here. Miramsita and I will herd the horses onto the truck. All of them are equipped to transport animals: the back gate folds down making an easy bridge onto the platform. I must go now but I will be back soon...so make sure you are ready!" The man left as quickly and silently as he had arrived.

Olga was noticeably nervous. "It is no use! They will catch up to us as soon as the weather calms. Anyway, you cannot even see the road in this weather."

It was Miramsita's turn to speak out. She had known her girlfriend for many years. "Do not worry. They will not tell your family much. It they do not apprehend us as expected, the Colonel will be busy saving his own skin. He will invent some story, like, hm, like.." searching for the right comparison the girl spent only a few seconds, "..like being overcome in a storm, or something to that effect. Remember, your father has very influential friends in Moskow. An arrest in itself will take time, preparation for representation. The KGB works differently. They will use extortion if they can but I am certain that they will not choose to do so. They can wait and simply tell that you were lost in a snowstorm crossing the highlands." Since the underlings of the different detachments were rarely suspect, they took the side of their immediate superior in most cases. This much Olga knew herself and the deliberations of her girlfriend began to make sense.

"We need our maps." Olga, who had obviously regained control of herself, was addressing all of them.

"I do not have them," replied Miramsita, now looking toward the Manchurian. "They are in your luggage Takuan," reminded the girl.

"Not in mine any longer," answered Takuan. "You took all of them, remember, in your shoulder bag."

"All right, hang onto them. I have a detailed group of maps from this region, they are all topographical ones," replied Olga. "They will do for the first days."

"But we don't have a worthwhile plan yet," reminded the Tiger his friends.

"If our Tamu can arrange for the truck we can move west for awhile, providing that we're able to connect to the main road. Our plan will only work if we can trick them, if we're better than they at this game of deceit," added the Manchurian. "We would be better off to go east, drop the truck near Tosontsengel and follow the river back west, ride along the banks of the Ideriyan. Anyway, my folks do not live in the Altai's, they were only born there: they live in the hills of Jargalant. Jargalant is near the river. It will be a hard go, but it might work. We all could winter there."

"All right then, let's do it!" began the Tiger to follow the suggestion of the Manchurian. The Mongolian girl could aid them in many ways. It was possible to outsmart the system if they would stick together. Not all that sticks is necessarily good but if trust can be made to stick it will when reared by danger. Olga knew that she would be blamed for the harboring of the Manchurian and the Cossack and Miramsita herself would be deemed a co-conspirator and so on. Either way, it would demand courage to escape from the clutches of the Secret Police. Freedom from persecution sounded to them more inviting than freedom through punishment. The plan was made. It would be perfected as time went on. Now, all that counted was to produce the perspicacity to beat the KGB in their own game, using the time given to them wisely. It should become one of the most remarkable feats of that time lingering on through the storytellers of the tribesmen for many generations to come.

The wind outside had grown into a storm, driving very dense masses of snow ahead of itself. The tent in which they were would not be staying up very much longer. Both men hurried to get their things from their own tent so that they could put all their gear together in one location. As they left in order to do so, they observed that the snow was being driven by the storm strong enough to lay perfectly horizontal in the air. The Colonel's structure was being pushed in from the northerly side, now requiring a much larger group of soldiers to work on it in a fervent attempt to stabilize it. The Colonel, however, did not show himself, leaving that responsibility to rest with his subordinates. The increasing confusion and excitement allowed Tamu to make his way to the trucks. Four of the GMC haulers were being used to confine the expedition's many horses. Tamu had to rearrange the vehicles in order to retrieve the animals. They formed a perfect square around them. The Mongolian agent began his work.

"Over here!" resounded his loud command to one of the soldiers nearest him. "Get the man who can drive this thing and put it into the wind! Don't have the trucks facing the west you idiot!" This particular soldier happened to be the driver of the unit.

"What about the horses?" yelled the driver.

"Don't worry about them. They know what to do. They're not going anywhere. Turn your truck into the wind, now!" The soldier followed the order, shouting something under his breath as he moved toward the truck.

Both friends used their time with great efficiency. As soon as they gathered their belongings, they left the tent and returned to the girls. The weather had established itself following the calls of nature, the wind ebbing, the gusts steadying themselves as the density of the snowfall increased. The storm began to drown out any existing noise, burying it within the snow squall.

"If it gets worse," speculated Olga, "they may come to ask us all to share one tent, put us all together."

"At the moment they seem to be in control of the situation. But you are correct," agreed the Tiger, "we might have to change our plans. Right now let's wait with that and..." His words were interrupted. The Manchurian pointed to the commotion where a pulling and tugging movement of the canvas indicated an attempt to

207

enter. The Tiger, being nearest, stepped close, carefully opening the latch straps which were hooked on the inside. It was Tamu. He slipped quickly inside.

"Everything is ready. I remembered three of your horses, the fourth one I was not sure of. I took another one, near the white and brown one, it had a bleached white tail."

"That is mine," began Miramsita. "You got mine!"

"We all better go together, leave our things here for the time being," suggested the Tiger. "Our concern about our animals should not arouse suspicion as long as we leave our stuff in the tent." The idea was at once accepted. Tamu, Olga, Miramsita and then finally followed by the two friends, a strange group of people began to depart. The storm had rested in its effort to some degree as if it wanted to become comfortable in its work. The dimly lit encirclement which the trucks had formed was difficult to spot. However, the one huge truck was busy repositioning itself. Its glaring headlights bounced off a wall of white ice crystals, producing the silhouette of the makeshift compound which now revealed a wide opening to the east. The horses, however, remained behind the wind barrier which the remaining trucks still offered. With swift and determined effort the five persons reached the site. It was here that Tamu made his move. He commanded two soldiers to help untie a few horses, telling them as soon as they had done so to report to the tent of the Colonel. The two friends were busy locating their saddles and their luggage all of which were well stored beneath a tarpaulin. The Cossack was the first to finish saddling his horse.

"I'll get our things!" was all he was able to yell into the

night as he mounted his horse in an instant, pressing his legs against its flanks, shooting across the icy distance.

The girls were soon ready as well, now following Tamu. Their animals were laden with all the essentials they were able to gather, riding through the night, aiming toward the gravel road which revealed itself from time to time since it clung to a dried out river bed, clearly showing a difference in the markings of the landscape. However, it would not be long before even that would disappear. The Mongolian agent had done his work. The truck was ready and Olga's horse was the first one to tred upon the wooden ramp. Miramsita's horse as well as Takuan's were just as quickly on the back of the huge box, Tamu waiting for the Cossack. As this proceeded, the orders of the Mongolian agent were being observed. Several other trucks were turned sideways to the wind. The activity was one which was important in any case. A snowdrift which lays itself sideways against the trailer box would be considerably larger than one which would fill the space, either at the rear or front. The hilly country was infamous for producing snowdrifts twenty meters high and the blizzards raging out here were known to last weeks. In but a few minutes the white, moving wall of snow was being divided by a dark shadow. The Cossack, high on horseback, had returned riding his animal directly onto the box of the truck. Dismounting swiftly, he aided his friends who were trying to tie their animals to a rail near the cab. The huge box was well framed with a corral-like, wooden rail. Their horses were safe. As soon as this task was behind them, they all left the deck, locking the rear gate. Tamu received a hardy hug from most of them. He was however very impatient, pushing each and every one of them away from him, urging them to move faster. The running truck was warm inside as they all squeezed into it, the Cossack now moving the monster, backing it up a few yards and then finally turning it into the raging blizzard. While rolling his window down he was able to exchange a few last words with Tamu, thanking him and, most of all, getting the final directions for the main road to Moeroen. It was only a half a kilometer away from them.

"It's about eighty kilometers from the road to Tosontsengel," explained the Cossack. Miramsita and Takuan were sitting directly beside him while Olga was pressed against the right side of the cabin. "This thing is filled with gas!" resumed the Cossack while he began to make the first, large turn on the small gravel road.

"Watch out! There's a big drop there!" pointed the Manchurian to his right side. A broken rail was sticking morbidly into the air. Avoiding it, they rolled slowly and carefully down a shallow stretch of road. As they followed it through the densely flying snow they suddenly reached the main road.

"God Almighty, this is it!" sighed Olga as a wide, flat band of snow covered ground, evenly flowing alike a white river, presented itself to them. The four friends had made the most important connection. They had reached the main road. For a few moments hope returned and Olga even began to sing, quietly humming a tune, interchanging the present excitement with some pleasant moment of the past.

With the snowstorm now coming from the west, it pushed the huge truck along, the white icy crystals storming in myriads over their cab, twirling icy dust ahead of them. At the same time, whenever an extreme gust came down, passing over them, gushing like a white river onto the street, its surface, the crude oiled gravel road, was being exposed. This alone made the trip possible.

"Man," started the Cossack, "are we lucky with the wind pushing us like this. It's plowing the road for us!"

Takuan looked at the gearshift handles. Two of them were side by side, one of them being higher than the other one. The smaller lever had many notches, sort of stages, marked beside it.

"You're going very slow, my friend," remarked Takuan, "you must still be in a low gear. Too much noise coming from the gear box."

"Yes," answered his friend, "I heard that too but I don't know how to shift higher. I don't know which gears do what!" A hair raising sound began to fill the space as their driver proceeded to experiment with the more *sophisticated* mechanism of the GMC truck.

"That's even further down. You've got to go the other way!" shouted his friend, pointing at the small lever. "That type, the short one, usually controls the lower range, sort of.."

"All right, all right!" answered the young Cossack. "So I'm using the clutch wrong, but I got the gear in, just the same. In any event, Takuan, the wheel turns really well, easy for a rig of this size. Look, we're making forty miles."

Suddenly, the headlights captured the silhouette of a parked vehicle. It was now up to their driver to miss it. As they approached the obstacle, they could see it was the front of a small car which had careened into a shallow ditch bordering the right side of the invisible road. The Cossack tried to step twice on the clutch

211

while he was shifting down and this time the gear fell much easier into place, the truck accepting the order without its usual bucking in resistance to the cruel treatment of the driver.

"We should make the next town in not less than two hours," announced Olga who had computed their speed and distance, knowing that Tosontsengel was only eighty kilometers away.

Takuan, in the meantime, studied the map which he had borrowed from Miramsita. He suddenly got an idea. As the situation was, Tamu somehow had to cover for the missing truck. Sooner or later the blizzard would have to come to an end. Why were the four leading persons of the caravan missing and where did they go? As Takuan posed his thoughts to his friends for discussion, they began to change their plan. In the outset, hurrying to get away and to avoid any given order, they were still under the previously valid instructions from Moskow. The Cossack was not participating very much in the discussion preferring to keep his attention on the road, observing the vehicle to the right of him as he passed it. It was snow covered and showed no sign of life. It would not have been prudent to stop in any event. Firstly, the Cossack was elated with the skill of achieving motion: in fact, having been able to move the rig from a standstill to a point where he was even negotiating a few hair raising turns. The act of halting the huge power base was as yet not a desirable feat. They also had to use their time wisely since their withdrawal from the camp imposed a problem, not only on the Colonel of the KGB but very much so on their present activities. After all, they borrowed a government truck without the permission of the person who was responsible for it. Miramsita sat quietly listening to the conversation. Momentarily, however, as soon as a particular thought entered her mind she shot up from her seat, which allowed her only centimeters of upward movement quickly reminding her to curtail this type of enthusiasm, bellowing away as if she had struck gold.

"We could drive it south, you know! Follow the gravel roads, then leave it there and continue alongside the Delger until we reach the road west of Moeroen again."

Takuan took another good, long look at the map which he still had spread out, resting between him and the volant, reaching forward and sideways covering the distance between him and the Cossack and Miramsita who was holding the other end of it. The Manchurian shook his head.

"Look, we want to go south. But here, we would be proceeding west. Using the same distance we can make it to Jargalant, see?" Miramsita's eyes followed as Takuan measured the distance from the point of confluence where both rivers met south of Tosontsengel.

Driving onward through the night, heading east, the storm still raged with the same intensity but it clearly did not carry the huge amount of snow any longer. It was, therefore, possible to shift into a faster gear, though still remaining in the lower range. As their *driver* managed to achieve the transfer, the truck lurched for a moment only to then behave very well afterwards. Everybody enjoyed this performance and now, for the first time, the Cossack began to speak, having paused for the longest interval.

"When I left, I pulled the stakes on the far side of the Colonel's tent since his crew was busy securing it on the windward side. I also removed the holding line from our tent so it'll flop and, over time, give way."

"Oh boy!" chuckled the Manchurian. "They'll be in dire straits by now!"

"Yes," giggled Miramsita, "the Colonel will have to find his *undees* with the wind blowing!"

"That bum will not run after anything! He will send his entire army after his underwear!" shouted Olga in anger. "I know his type!"

Having thus injected some humor into the affair, the truck went on, missing at times a row of bushes or passing with its rear end through a ditch, bouncing the horses about, giving them a measure of their own habits. As the truck thumped its way east, several hours had quickly gone by. A few huts appeared on either side of the road, while the first glimmer of light showed itself directly ahead of them. Olga mentioned that it must be Tosontsengel. At this very moment the Cossack began to shift downward, succeeding brilliantly, slowing the vehicle from the forty mile mark to the line reading twenty miles, happy to have gotten the monster under control. As the light came closer their hearts began to speed up.

"All right, here we go!" said the driver. Approaching with great caution, the long vehicle had slowed to but a crawl. The first bright lights were right of them, glaring over an open space which was being literally pounded upon by the gusting wind, carrying corrugated metal sheets along its path of destruction. The Cossack decided to halt his rig and pushed the clutch to the floor, shifting, trying to find the spot which would stop it moving. Each and every time that he was confident he had succeeded the thing began to

214

jump, telling him that he as yet had not found the right notch. This enterprise continued for several minutes until finally the engine kept running without being engaged to its transmission: the beast had come to a standstill.

"This.." cautioned the Manchurian, "I think, is not a good spot to stop! Too much light, too close to the building and that thing looks too much like an official structure. Look at the red star on the top." Everybody soon saw the red star and began to feel very depressed. The Cossack was busy trying to make the thing move. For the first time he had to find the reverse gear in order to swing the front of the vehicle around sufficiently to avoid some serious obstacles. The storm was beginning to show its nasty side again shaking on the structure of the truck. Countless debris of one sort or other rolled over the open space as if the storm itself was being encouraged by its own actions, pushing and tearing away at the snow covered ground. Miramsita decided to listen to her radio. Clipping the earphones over her head, she removed her fur cap until her long black hair fell on Takuan's shoulder, reminding him that they both had decided to break free from the fearful surrounding of a state which governed its citizens by cunning, leading them in a circle, a never ending road offering dismay, separation and suffering for those who wished to think for themselves. One had to think like the rest. Political thought had to be the same, no deviation, no altering or change was allowed without that permission was given, approved and documented.

"Hold it!" shouted the Mongolian girl suddenly, her hand pushing Takuan's arm away from her. "They are calling for assistance! The Colonel's people are on the air." This announcement was important enough for the driver to halt the vehicle totally, cutting the noise of the engine by turning the key, killing it. During the very same moment many quick words of excitement crossed the cabin. Miramsita removed one of the earphones so Takuan was able to listen into the conversation. The Cossack and Olga knew that this was no time to ask questions. It was important that they did not miss any of the exchanged information which was of significant value to their immediate decision making.

"What're they saying?" interrupted the anxious Cossack no longer able to curtail his patience.

"Wait, wait.. quiet!" was all he was able to get as an answer from the girl. These were frustrating seconds, portentous to their future as they were, they appeared to last and last and last again.

Then, after a few thousand moments, the girl began to talk. "They are off the air. Their batteries must have gone dead. The words just faded away. Their tents went with the wind and the snow has apparently covered everything. They were speaking of drifts of two meters. It was not the Colonel but someone who was able to operate it."

"I saw one Jeep with a radio antenna," said the Tiger who was resting his body on the large circle of the steering wheel.

"Of course," continued Takuan, "they parked in that depression, down from our tent. It would, no doubt in my mind, fill faster with snow than a hundred shovels can shovel."

"Enough about them, comrades," said Olga finally losing patience, "are they looking for us, did they miss us? Any word about that?"

"No, nothing of that at all," answered the Manchurian, who was able to hear each and every word as well.

"They said the temperature has dropped to minus fifteen Celsius," added Miramsita.

"Well, it looks as if they are blocked in by the snowdrifts. Without their tent covering them, they are in deep trouble!" concluded Olga.

"Anything else, was there anything else you heard on that thing?" queried the Cossack.

"No, not really, other than that they were asking for assistance. They need help in the worst way. The operator was actually calling a mayday. I guess he should have given the coordinates first. There is little we can do." As soon as the girl reported her last impressions, the Cossack, as if shot by a cannon, jumped from where he was and left the truck, the cabin door almost breaking off. Fortunately, the alert man kept it under control, wrestling with it for an instant only, before closing it. He made his way to the rear of the vehicle, took a look at it and, as rapidly and wildly as he had departed, he managed to return. The cab door flew open only to be shut again after a great struggle, Takuan sliding from the bench to the door opening, trying to assist his friend, closing it finally.

"What on earth's going on?" Takuan yelled out his question while they were struggling to close the cab door, the howling wind swallowing each and every syllable of his words.

"Look up there, the red star!" shouted the Cossack, pointing to the top of the huge complex on which some lanterns blazed their bright light into the night making it difficult to see past them.

217

"Yea, we all saw it! It's still there!" taunted Takuan, having seen it before, everyone talking about it.

"Look again!" said his friend, trying this time to bring his excitement under better control. "There, beneath it is a sign. Don't you see it yet?"

"Okay, I see it now," answered the Manchurian. "It's mounted on a knight's shield, light blue or grey, right? Showing an arm, the hand holding a sort of stick!"

"Right on, my friend!" roared the Cossack triumphantly, "That's not a stick but a bundled group of sort of lightning flashes held by a hand. It's the same damn sign which we have on the back of this truck!"

"You're kidding, you're...you don't say!" said the Manchurian rather hesitantly, not yet understanding.

"I have an idea," the Cossack continued eagerly again. "Let's find out who lives behind that sign up there."

"Well, obviously it is the same outfit!" the irritation in Olga's voice becoming quite apparent.

"Not necessarily," replied the Tiger. "Remember, Tamu said that they *arranged* for them."

"Well, what does that mean? For goodness sake, what are you trying to tell us?" Miramsita's voice was now beginning to show her irritation also. However, the young Tiger had no quick reply.

"The way I see it is this," resumed the Cossack slowly. "We can turn a disadvantage into an advantage. If they are who I think they are, they'll listen to us." As the man paused for a brief moment everyone in the cab asked the same question at the same

218

time.

"Who are *they*?"

"Never mind, right now, I'll come to that later," came the hurried answer from the Tiger. He then began to reveal his thoughts to his friends and explained his entire plan which had come to him in just a few moments. The tactical sign on the back of the truck indicated that the vehicle belonged to a special military unit. They, all of them, having fled because of Tamu's warning were, in fact, fleeing from prosecution. Since the Colonel had not arrested them, for whatever reason he must have had, he could hardly announce that they fled to avoid an arrest which had as yet not taken place. If the group could make contact with an authority and send help to the camp, telling that they overheard the mayday message which was void of the position, it was realistic that they could continue, for awhile at least, pretending that they were on their previous mission. The order of the Colonel to remain under his authority was not really valid. The fact remained that they were a civilly empowered expedition corps, properly documented and equipped, moving about in order to engage in specific scientific research. After the Cossack explained his idea, silence prevailed. They had arrived at the crossroads of their planned escape. Miramsita was the first who saw the advantage of his plan and simply announced: "That is brilliant and it will work and we get time and opportunity along with it. Our options here, right now, are lousy ones!"

"Fantastic, my friend!" applauded Takuan. "It's great, it'll work, I know it. It will!"

"The position, his position.." added Miramsita. "He did not have to give me one. Remember Takuan, the aircraft, he talked about the Delger airstrip."

"Of course! We couldn't see it any longer. That was the big white looking strip where the wood was sticking up, the railing."

The discussion which subsequently ensued solved the one major flaw in their plan. Since they were able to relate to a specific location, one which was absolutely identifiable, they would be able to go on with this plan: and this was the most important point, otherwise it would be expected of them to return to the spot in question, thus inviting all of them back into the same perilous situation from which they daringly escaped. There was no reason now to take them back in order to find the spot, at least not if they were talking about the grass airstrip near where the camp was established. The only problem the four friends now had was a procedural one. Who was going to make the initial contact and, most of all, did the complex indeed harbor any living soul. It was two o'clock in the morning, long past midnight. The storm had as yet not awakened the citizens. They either slept like Vodka drinkers or the town, if it was indeed already the town, was deserted.

"I think I'll knock on some doors and see..." offered the Manchurian, deciding to use the stalled moment in order to make some progress.

Olga interrupted his thoughts, "You are not the right person for this. I have the propusk and if I tell them that I chose to drive away to get help, being a woman, and that makes a difference here, we will get some action."

"Maybe if I go, being of the people, knowing the dialect, I can make a difference," volunteered Miramsita.

"Why don't you both go," proposed the Tiger. "Offer them

this rig here. They can have it after we take our gear down and.."
The man looking on the map, which still lay on the dash, appeared
to have an extra thought. Pausing long enough to be able to
formulate it, he went on to explain, "If we tell them that we're
riding towards Il Uul but instead leave from here not going east but
southwest, we'll have them off our backs for awhile at least!"

"…and…" resumed Miramsita, "make it downhill, not from
the closest point of the Selenge but aiming straight for the fork of
the Delger and Ideriyin."

"Sounds good to me!" replied the Manchurian, adding, that
it would take them four days of hard work to reach Jargalant. "The
river doesn't flow much during this part of the year," explained
Takuan to his friends, telling of the time he had spent there many
years ago. The place was about sixty kilometers north of Jargalant.
His folks operated a river barge which primarily served as a ferry
near the first large bend north of the town. He spoke of the major
turns the river made from the southern most confluence of the
Selenge. Coming from the north, they had to observe three big
curves, watching at the beginning of the third bend for the signs of
a ferry service. The landing itself was as yet another eight
kilometers from their home, going east, reaching the slope of the
Tavagatain Nuuru Range, the northerly most ridge which makes up
the valley between the western one, almost three thousand meters
high.

The Tiger began to move the truck closer to the building,
close enough to observe it more accurately. Crossing over the large
space, they went to the blind side of the structure where a huge iron
fence separated the town from the storage compound. As the group

221

scrutinized the site, they soon learned what they were dealing with.

"Will you look at that!" began the Mongolian girl, "Lots of tanks, hundreds of them!" They had indeed stumbled onto a military storage depot. The Cossack turned his rig around so fast he almost clipped the steel fence as he made his getaway from the site. In doing so, he again passed across the huge square in an effort to reach the main road again. As the Tiger was concentrating on missing trees and curbstones which came dangerously close to his path, he received a sharp elbow blow from his friend, strong enough not only to get his attention but to shock him.

"Over there! They've made us! Jeeps and cars.." Having not even finished his outcry the whole lot of them began to encircle the truck, armed personnel leaping at them from all directions.

"Oh no.." was all Olga was able to utter while the first soldier had already begun to open the cab door where Olga was seated.

"Go ahead, open it!" whispered the Tiger. "We've nothing to hide." As soon as Olga released the handle, the man outside pulled the door open.

"What the hell are you gallivanting about for? I am Captain Kashvili, Quarter Master Detachment."

"Look at the back of our vehicle, Comrade. We just came from the Delger airstrip and barely made the road. You have thirty men there stranded in a blizzard. When the tent collapsed we were closest to the road and free of snowdrifts so we just took off to look for a relief party. We're exhausted Comrade Captain!"

"And who precisely are you, Comrade?" asked the officer in return, noticeably easing the tension which prevailed.

222

"We are scientists on special orders of the Ministry of the Interior in Moskow. I am Olga Likhavchev and this here.." Olga casually pointing to her girlfriend, "is Dr. Miram Fiehsueh, though she actually goes by her Mongolian name."

"I see," smiled the officer for the first time. "My grandmother is Chinese as well. Fiehsueh, flying snow, right?"

"It is flying all right Comrade," replied Miramsita.

"Yes. Well let's get with it!" prompted the officer. "I can arrange for a party to depart in ten minutes. You said the Delger airstrip?"

"That is correct Comrade." Olga began to take over the conversation once more. "We drove in less than marginal conditions though," came her introduction to the state of affairs as they had presented themselves to the four friends.

"Well, it's only an hour's drive from here," replied the officer, standing within the space the widely opened cab door offered, blasting the cold air across the inside of the enclosure. "All right, follow me into the compound. We'll look after your stay and send a group to the strip."

With this final comment the officer left, waving his vehicle close and leaving in it, the window rolled down, gesturing to follow him. The Cossack began to crank the engine, waiting for it to respond, then, shifting mightily, proceeded to follow the officer. After a few hundred meters they saw a meagrely lit gate at which the *"pilot"* car stopped, someone leaving it. Within a short time bright, massive light began to illuminate a huge section of the compound. Guard dogs appeared, dozens of them, accompanied by their handlers. The big steel gate began to roll open. It moved

223

sideways to their right. The Cossack had a difficult time maneuvering the sharp S-curve. He could clear the gate, which was wide enough all right, but after it a large concrete structure asked for avoidance, a feat which provided not only the optimum challenge but supreme skill. At this moment, the Cossack left the cab asking Olga to come along. Olga then was able to tell the officer in charge that the driver had volunteered to drive the truck in order to make the trip possible but that he was not equipped to squeeze it past "these obstacles here". Having made her statement the officer produced the biggest smile yet. This same officer now proceeded to jump into the big GMC truck and, backing it up, left it parked parallel to the fence outside the compound. This was exactly what the Tiger had hoped for. They had now succeeded in placing the vehicle under a new state of ownership. They only had to remove their horses, rest awhile, then get going and Olga's modern maps would accomplish the rest! For the moment, the officer was busy arranging their overnight stay.

"We should offer the truck to them," whispered Miramsita.

"Let's first get the horses under control and not give them the idea that they're for hire. This truck alone won't get the men out of their misery at the airstrip; however, the truck and the horses combined might," cautioned Takuan.

As they were talking, remaining inside the cab, waiting for the events to unfold, the Tiger had again taken his place behind the wheel. The officer passed through the gate and talked to some of his men. After a short while they began to scurry about until the small group of men dispersed, leaving the officer and two of his men remaining. Then, one of the men began to walk over to their truck approaching Olga's side.

"A weather warning has just been issued, calling for forty-eight hours of mayhem. Strong winds and low temperatures coupled with intense snow are to dominate this entire area. You better leave your truck right here and come along with me. We have some room behind the compound in the guards' quarters."

The four friends hurried to collect their things. A parked Jeep turned on its lights and began to move towards their truck. It was ready to pick them up, swerving sideways in front, coming to a full stop. They had succeeded in setting a rescue mission into operation: they were able to get rest and sleep; and personnel were even being sent to feed their horses. The animals were to remain on the rear of the truck. They were well protected from the wind but not from the falling snow, which fortunately for the moment had ceased. There was still a large amount of it in the air but it was the drifting type not fed by new, additional quantities of moisture. Soon all four friends found themselves driving about in the Jeep, the soldier maneuvering it alongside the long fence, wheeling in a very large circle around the far side of it, aiming for a well lit, two story building. Clouds of twirling snow, debris and scooting veils of ice dust brushed over the snow covered pavement quickly uncovering the surface and then just as rapidly hiding it. The storm, which had relaxed its activity for awhile, appeared to be gaining strength again as if it had needed a rest to recover. At the guardhouse a group of men left its sheltered walls in order to assist the arriving party. Within only a few moments they all were safely inside.

Once the door shut behind them they could see the space

225

was well lit; brightly shining lamps, in double rows, hanging from long wire strings spread the light from beneath funnel-like, green colored shades. A handful of soldiers, dressed in their fatigues, made room for the women as they introduced themselves. Takuan and his friend, whom he proudly described as being a Cossack, began to exchange the well established courtesies. Hot tea, food of all sorts was being served to the four rescuers. The word had spread, the group of four had managed to break away from the endangered airstrip. A soldier, arriving from an office which was somewhere further inside the building, brought the news that a Siberian High, one which carried outflow winds, was expected to settle in for the next few days. Temperatures would fall to ten or fifteen degrees below Celsius. The wind had been forecast to increase to more than a hundred kilometers an hour. The soldier announced that the news was being transmitted by an American weather station some two hundred kilometers from them. The Americans had an agreement with the Soviets during the Great War and would be, at least so the soldier reported, vacating the station they had built in the early part of the coming year. The interaction found each of the friends separately engaged. The atmosphere was a happy one and very constructive for the four. Miramsita learned much about the Ideriyn River. A soldier told her that a comfortable path existed which leads all the way downhill to the Delger River, right from their town to where the boats are anchored. He mentioned as well, after being casually asked, that the distance was close to thirty kilometers. Olga and the Mongolian girl were to share common quarters for the remainder of the night while the Manchurian and the Cossack would stay in the same hall in which most of the guards slept. Takuan was able to get closer to Miramsita under the pretense of asking for pieces of his luggage. She quickly related the story the soldier had told her. The Manchurian made the decision that they would all prepare to leave at the onset of daylight, regardless of the weather. Upon returning, the Manchurian brought the news to his friend.

"It's only a day's ride from here to the Delger...and..get this...this one soldier dates a girl somewhere near where a boat is supposed to be moored, a motor boat of some sort." Concluding so, they proceeded to observe, with great caution, those who were near to them. Both men reasoned that if the blizzard would only last an extra day instead of two or even three days, as the weather prediction said, they would be far out of range. It was now important to tell these guards a different story, giving them the idea that they were going toward the east, attempting to reach Il Uul. They would have to plant information which was in line with their story.

The time had already advanced to the early morning hours and none of them would be able to get the rest they needed to continue. The storm began to shake the building again, fallen debris began to bang about causing unrest amongst the soldiers who were entrusted with the safety of the compound.

It was not before long that the four friends were back together, having their breakfast. They had calculated that the rescue mission could occur within a five hour time span. Since little snow was falling in Tosontsengel, one could reason that the airstrip, which was not too far away from them, had also seen the worst of the snow. After all, it was the falling snow, coupled by strong winds, which had created drifts of monumental height. A few soldiers appeared, bundled in arctic parkas, one of them separating from the rest, approaching the table around which the four friends were seated eating and drinking all that was given to them.

"Good morning, Comrades. The Captain sent me to tell you that our mission is stuck about four kilometers short of the airfield. The drifts which are blocking the road there are four meters high. That's twice the size of a person!" explained the messenger. He was a rather young Mongolian soldier, happy and forthcoming in nature.

Takuan answered him, showing interest in his report saying, "They might be able to reach them on foot, Comrade. The group has food and appeared to have heating stoves, from what I could tell. Talking to Colonel Nakhimov, he did not give me the impression that he was in a hurry, at least not when we were at their camp."

As soon as the soldier heard the word Nakhimov his interest waned, telling that that that *"guy"* was a sort of careless individual, always demanding attention.

"By the way, Comrade," interjected the Tiger, wanting to now change the topic, "we have to get to our horses. They'll be in need of food by now."

"Oh no Comrade, they are quite all right. I saw the boys feeding them just awhile ago when I was passing the grain shed."

"You have a grain shed here amidst all the heavy armor?" asked the Manchurian.

"Oh yes, we are the emergency supply depot for all of Mongolia. Everybody knows that around here! If we don't have it no one does!" boasted the man.

228

Before the soldier was able to proceed about his business, Olga addressed him saying that it would help to know how to get to the shed.

"Comrade," he said, "it has started to snow really heavy out there. The wind can knock you down. But if you really do want to go, make sure to stay close to the side of the building and avoid the fence. You'll be in the wind shadow if you stay with the building. At the end of it, you'll see a very high light standard, the only one there, that's if you turn hard right as soon as you leave the second side door. It'll tell you the direction to the munitions depot. You follow that and the shed is right, that is right from where the big lamp stands. You can see the open side of the shed. You'll be able to see the horses from there." The young man was attempting to remove himself while still speaking, glancing for a few seconds in the direction where he wanted to go then turning back towards the person to whom he was conversing, attaching himself to where he had been. The soldier was obviously in a hurry using this method of disengagement to detach himself from the source which kept him unduly occupied.

Having learned much about their situation, the four of them decided that it was time to move on. Since they had managed to retain almost all of their own essential equipment, dried food, solid fuel and down filled, waterproof, all-weather wear, none of them hesitated making certain, based on the information given to them, not to waste too much time. In the meantime, the morning hours had advanced considerably. Takuan began to press for their departure, reminding his girlfriend to make Olga understand that they must use the time available to them very wisely. After all, it would still take them a full day to reach the river. If the weather conditions would improve earlier than the predicted duration of the very blizzard which had brought them their freedom, the same opportunity could be easily lost.

Within the next half hour the caravan was back in business. The horses were saddled, the bags strapped to the respective animals and all of the riders mounted. It was time to depart. As they were about to leave the shed the Captain came to say good-bye. He cautiously drove his Jeep as close as possible and shook the hands of Olga, talked to her, than reached up to Miramsita, tugged jokingly at her parka, tapping the horse on his hind quarters as he wished her well. He had a few hardy words for the men and thanked the group for stopping.

"Watch out on the main road. I hear you are heading east. You should actually not go but- then, everybody has to go on with their mission." Having said that, he waited a short while, standing near the shed, protected from the howling wind as he watched the four comrades move into the weather.

It was not before long when the first gust touched the lead rider. It was Takuan. Millions of icy snow crystals began to strike the exposed portions of his face making the horse lower its head in order to better brave the crosswind which now had an easy time with man and beast alike having left the protective shelter of the walls of the compound. Olga and her girlfriend had spent enough time getting directions to assure all of them that they knew the correct street in order to find the feeder road toward the path which would bring them to the banks of the big river. Their Mongolian horses were a godsend. The animals proved to have a hardiness bordering on the miraculous. They were capable of sustaining themselves indefinitely as long as the snow was not too high. Any blade of grass which reached above that level was food for them. Before the animals would starve, they would begin to forage for grass, scraping the surface until they had uncovered the layer of snow which was hiding the food from them. Many noted, modern day expeditions learned quickly that the icy regions cannot readily be conquered by modern machinery. The Norwegian explorer refused to use the motor sled preferring to rely upon the dog sled. As the world realized later, he had made the right decision.

Takuan was followed by an extra pack horse and then by his Mongolian girlfriend and Olga, who were being closely pursued by the Tiger who himself was followed by another pack horse. They had sufficient supplies to last them for two weeks, bad weather and all. With each and every stride the horses were able to make, the noose, which was being held by the KGB, began to loosen. Miramsita had spoken to Takuan about her family in Kumul. A good hundred kilometers from there was an ancient temple, teaching a survival method which had inspired many young Mongolian wrestlers. Yet, according to Miramsita, they had no one who was able to recommend them in order to enter it. The Manchurian needed to stay away from China for obvious reasons. The Japanese occupation was as yet not forgotten and - most of all- the civil war in China was still heating up. The Sinkiang Province was sparsely populated and offered harsh living conditions. Kumul was a fair sized city for that region, yet it was poorly governed, suffering from the struggle which had been concentrating all efforts toward Western China. The *"Tigers of Sinkiang"* were the monks who

231

ruled within the forgotten population, filling a void at a time when the great struggle passed them by. The Mongolian girl knew of her uncle who had lived many years in that Temple. She hoped that the four friends could reach it and remain there until the veils of time would hush their past.

This ADVENTURE SERIES is continued in sequence as outlined below and should be read in consecutive order to be understood.

Volume I - The White Priest
Volume II - Takuan the Manchurian
Volume III - The Tigers of Sinkiang
Volume IV - The Lost Jade
Volume V - The Living Arrow
Volume VI - The Soul of Emptiness
Volume VII - The Borders of Heaven
Volume VIII - Reincarnation of the Tiger

Other books by O.E. Simon:

Novels: Shalom
                     Curse of the Gods

Poetry: Book of Thought
                     Book of Hope
                     Book of Life
                     Book of Destiny

Technical Work: The Law of the Fist
                     Anti-Rape & Total Self-Defense

Books can be individually ordered from:

In Canada: Golden Bell Publishing House Inc.
               P.O. Box 2680
               Grand Forks, B.C. V0H 1H0

In US: Golden Bell Publishing House Inc.
               P.O. Box 181
               Danville, Washington 99121-0181

or orders may be placed through your local bookstore.

About the Author

Being the product of a Europe in war, the author saw both man at his best and at his worst. After surviving the prison camps and the post-war agonies, though educated in Germany, receiving a National literary prize for his Dornberger Hexameter, the author decided to seek out a new country where he could work, dream and hope to be a part of a new and better future for mankind.

Now internationally known, he remains a citizen of Canada living in seclusion, still travelling, writing, teaching the philosophy he has ascribed to for most of his life.